"I'm not your bride yet!"

He let go of her wrist, a tight smile twisting his lips into the semblance of humor. "You will be mine! I mean to have you, my Eleanor, flesh of my flesh, bone of my bone! How it will be is up to you, but have you I will. Make up your mind to it, you'll not escape me."

Her eyes were furious. "Haven't you done enough harm already?" she demanded.

"Tonight is mine," he insisted. "If you want it to be, it can be yours too, but willing or reluctant, tonight you become my bride of the sun."

ELIZABETH HUNTER

uses the world as her backdrop. She paints with broad colorful strokes, yet she is meticulous in her eye for detail. Well-known for her warm understanding of her delightful characters, she is internationally beloved by her loyal and enthusiastic readers.

Dear Reader:

Silhouette Romances is an exciting new publishing venture. We will be presenting the very finest writers of contemporary romantic fiction as well as outstanding new talent in this field. It is our hope that our stories, our heroes and our heroines will give you, the reader, all you want from romantic fiction.

Also, *you* play an important part in our future plans for Silhouette Romances. We welcome any suggestions or comments on our books and I invite you to write to us at the address below.

So, enjoy this book and all the wonderful romances from Silhouette. They're for *you!*

Karen Solem
Editor-in-Chief
Silhouette Books
P.O. Box 769
New York, N.Y. 10019

ELIZABETH HUNTER
Bride of the Sun

Silhouette Romance

Published by Silhouette Books New York

America's Publisher of Contemporary Romance

Other Silhouette Romances by Elizabeth Hunter

The Lion's Shadow

SILHOUETTE BOOKS, a Simon & Schuster Division of
GULF & WESTERN CORPORATION
1230 Avenue of the Americas, New York, N.Y. 10020

ISBN-0-671-57051-X

First Silhouette printing December, 1980

10 9 8 7 6 5 4 3 2 1

Bride
of the Sun

Chapter One

Eleanor Stewart was not given to feeling sorry for herself. Nor was she usually a lonely person, so when both emotions threatened to overwhelm her at one and the same time, she naturally thought it was the fault of the place where she found herself. Restively, she moved round the small house that had been her great-uncle's. There was much to admire in it, but little that was either labour-saving or modern. It was an ancient, traditional house of that district of the island. Her great-uncle, a man she remembered as fierce of manner and with the villainous looks of the pirates he had willingly claimed to be his ancestors, had kept it exactly as it had been built and furnished in his father's, or perhaps even in his grandfather's, time.

The house ran down two sides of a courtyard at the bottom of which was a primitive form of lavatory. There were two rooms, the main room being slightly larger than the lesser room. Standing in the doorway of either room there was a sleeping platform on the right-hand side, known as the *sophas,* and on the left-hand side were several chests used for storing clothes and other household articles. There was a minimum of other furniture, but the walls were richly covered with wooden planks carved into the shapes of strange animals and an impressive array of plates, pictures and embroidery. The effect was pretty, but, in Eleanor's opinion, impossible to live in.

The best part of the house, in her opinion, was the courtyard. The flooring had been done in a technique known as *chocklaki,* a kind of pebble pavement set in cement. In this case, different coloured sea pebbles had been used in an unusual design that was a constant delight to her. The other good thing about it was its privacy. The only way she could possibly be seen was from the house next door and that had been empty ever since her arrival. She was hopeful that it would remain that way.

Standing in the doorway to the courtyard she could see the sea, ultramarine, indeed almost black, the edges whipped pure white by the breeze. She was waiting for the estate agent who had promised to come that afternoon. She felt guilty about selling the place but what else could she do? She couldn't live in Rhodes for the rest of her life—it was the last thing she wanted to do if the isolation of the last few days was anything to go by!—but she did feel bad about transforming her great-uncle's gift into money.

Still, she comforted herself, the islanders were living more and more on their tourist industry. Hotels would have to be built to accommodate the swarms of visitors who wanted to come to Rhodes for their holidays. It would be of great benefit to everyone to have a hotel sited in this bay.

"*Kalispera.*" A male voice interrupted her thoughts. It was a deep voice and it held an intimate familiarity that startled her.

"*Kalispera sas,*" she answered awkwardly. Her Greek was almost nonexistent. Although her mother had learned Greek to please her own mother, Eleanor had been too far removed from the old lady to have made a similar effort to please her.

"You are English," the voice discovered in only very slightly accented tones. "You must be the old man's niece. I have been expecting you."

"Have you?" She was doubly intrigued now. "My great-uncle died—"

"He was dying when I went away," the voice confirmed. "But it was already arranged for you to come."

Eleanor raised herself on tiptoes and tried to peer over the wall between the two courtyards. "Where are you?" she demanded.

There was a smile in the voice as it answered. "Up on the roof. Look up and you will see me."

His hair was black and he was deeply tanned by the sun, but it was his eyes that she noticed most of all. They were a light greeny-grey and they shone like two pools of light in his brown, weather-beaten face.

"You've seen the sun!" she exclaimed before she could stop herself.

"Of course," he returned, amused, "Rhodes belongs to the sun. Haven't you discovered that for yourself?"

"It's been hot," she agreed. "But I thought Rhodes meant 'rose,' or something like that."

"Rodos was a nymph who caught the attention of the sun. He made her his bride and brought her to his island, which was named after her."

She was unsure of her mythology and, as she didn't want to demonstrate her ignorance on such a short acquaintance, she contented herself with a nod and the comment that most of the girls of the ancient world seemed to have fallen for Apollo.

"True, but Apollo was the god of light and brilliance. Helios was the god of the sun. He was out riding in his chariot when Zeus divided up the lands amongst the inhabitants of Olympus and Helios was forgotten. With unusual fairness, Zeus regretted the oversight, but Helios solved the problem for himself by causing the island to rise up above the sea. Scientists will tell you it was an earthquake that actually caused Rhodes to climb out of the waves and to deposit shells and fossils in the high hills, but don't you believe them. It was Helios who did it. Nor are you the first to confuse him with Apollo—the Rhodians have been doing it themselves since the beginning of time."

"I'll try and remember," she said solemnly. It was nice to have someone to talk to, even if he did talk a lot of nonsense. "I suppose you are a Rhodian?"

"I, too, was related to the old man," he told her. "More distantly than you are, but still a relation of sorts. That is why we came to the agreement between us. Neither of us wanted one of the houses to go out of the family."

"But it has to! Don't you see? *I* can't stay here forever. Whatever would I do with myself? Besides, I'm waiting for the agent now. They want the land for a new hotel. It will be a fine site for it, won't it?"

He shook his head. "It will never be." He paused, watching her closely with those fantastic eyes of his. She found his scrutiny embarrassing and wished she could return it with a like frankness. Instead, she fingered a flower that was growing out of the wall beside her.

"But I have to sell it!" she said. "I don't want a house in Rhodes. What on earth would I do with it?"

"It was all decided by the old man before you came," the man answered her gently. "It was agreed between us. Didn't your father—or maybe your mother—tell you why you were to come to Rhodes?"

"To sell the house!" she maintained stubbornly.

"Then they deceived you," he said more gently still. "The house is yours, but only as your *prika* or dowry. You cannot sell it, no matter how much you should want to do so."

11

"But nobody told me that!" she wailed. "And what should I do with a dowry? Nobody I'm likely to marry will want a house here in Rhodes! It hasn't even got a modern stove! In fact I haven't had a square meal since I got here!"

He laughed. "Poor Eleanor! Come round to my house and I will give you something to eat."

"Well, I might do just that! The shop in the village doesn't have much to sell that I feel competent to ask for, and half the things they do sell I don't know how to prepare!" She hesitated, eyeing him through her long lashes. "You seem to know my name," she went on, "but I'm afraid I don't know who you are," she apologized.

"I am Ioannis." He saw the bewilderment on her face and threw her a sympathetic smile. "Ioannis Nikkolides." His expression of sympathy changed to one of open mockery. "My full name is Ioannis Hyperion Nikkolides."

"I suppose Ioannis is the same as John," she said, feeling she ought to say something. "Hyperion sounds very ancient Greek to me."

"It is," he agreed, savouring the moment on his tongue. "Hyperion was his name in the Odyssey. He was the Sun-Titan, sometimes known as Helios."

"You mean you're named for the sun!" she exclaimed. "Isn't that rather—rather pagan?"

"Most Greek names are pagan in origin. Does it shock you?"

"No," she said at once, though it did rather. Not because he should have a pagan name as such, but because he should have been named after the god of the sun.

"Hyperion!" she scoffed. "I suppose they called you that because you were born in Rhodes?"

"Possibly. They called my sister Selene after the moon. It suits her very well. She is gentle and kind, just like the light of the full moon in summer."

Eleanor thought his own name sufficiently apt. He smelt of the sun and the sea; the paleness of his eyes in his dark, tanned face made her think of light and warmth—

"I'm glad you have a Christian name too!" she murmured. "I prefer Ioannis."

"Then you had better call me that," he invited her. "I shall call you Eleanor."

Now why in the world should that embarrass her? But it did. She was very conscious of the way he was looking at her, but she hadn't the courage to object. Only, it made her feel very feminine and not at all like her usual calm, decided self. On the contrary, when she met his eyes she could feel a distinct flutter somewhere in her middle. She looked hastily away again to give herself time to recover.

"Are you staying long?" she asked him when she could be sure she had regained control of her voice.

"As long as it takes."

"Oh," That had told her nothing at all. "How did you get here?"

He pointed out to sea. "You see the *caique* in the bay?"

"The one with rust-red sails?"

He nodded. "I came on that. If you can swim that far I'll take you out to see her sometime."

She was pleased. "I've always wanted to sail in one of those. They have such lovely lines, haven't they?"

"Of course. That one was Rhodian built. We have always had a name for navigation. We probably inherited our skills from the Phoenicians. If you would care to come out with me, you would be quite safe!"

"I'd come with you even if I weren't!" she said frankly, her eyes shining. "Where could we go? Right round the island?"

"If you like. I think I'll take you to Lindos. You will soon see that Rhodes has much to offer and then you'll no longer regret not being able to sell your house. You may even decide to live in it yourself!"

She made a face. "I doubt it."

He swung himself down from the roof of the next-door house, dropping lightly down into his own courtyard. "You say that because you are hungry," he said with a laugh. "Everything will look quite different to you on a full stomach. Come and see where I live and I shall do my poor best to make a feast for you to celebrate our meeting." He came out of his own gateway and looked at her, an eyebrow raised. "It is a matter for celebration, don't you think?"

She thought perhaps it was. "If you're going to feed me, it certainly is!" she said aloud.

He gave her a lopsided smile. "Naturally I shall feed you, and care for you, and look after you. Did you doubt it?"

"Well, I don't see why you should, but I shall be very grateful for a good meal. No matter how hard I've tried, I can't produce so much as a fried egg on that abominable grate in my house!"

"You will soon learn how to manage," he soothed her.

"Not if I can help it! Besides, whatever you say, the agent is coming this afternoon and I'm signing the house over to him." For the first time it occurred to her that the hotel was going to be uncomfortably close to his own house and she turned towards him in quick apology. "Won't you sell too? It can't be convenient for you to live here, and the agents are being more than generous in the price they are giving me. Please, won't you consider selling too?"

He took her hand in his. "Come and eat," he said. "I shall fry you some squid and some potatoes and make you a Greek salad. How will that be?"

She was uncertain about the squid. "I've never tried it," she confessed. "I thought it was sold for fishing bait."

He was amused. "You have seen it in the shops?"

She shook her head. "I saw a fisherman with some in his boat. They looked rather horrid, as a matter of fact."

"But taste delicious!" He stood back to allow her to precede him into the main room of his own house. It was very like her own, except where her own was so tidy that it had an impersonal air like a hotel bedroom, his showed every sign of being lived in. A half-empty bottle of wine stood on the table, a great pile of food beside it, and the fire burned brightly in the grate, showing none of the sulkiness that she associated with her own cooking facilities.

Ioannis hooked a chair out from under the table with his foot. "Sit down!" he bade her. "You will feel more at home when you've eaten my bread and tasted my salt."

And felt his warmth! The idea came to her unbidden. He emanated warmth just like the sun after whom he'd been named. Perhaps Hyperion did suit him better than Ioannis after all.

She sat down on the chair, clasping her hands on her knee as she looked about her. The furnishings were as charmingly folksy as her own, but here they had the aura of use. Even the water cooler was properly damp, but then perhaps he had a better idea than she did of how to use it. *She* had never been without a refrigerator in her whole life before!

It was only then that she noticed the crowing cock on the windowsill. It was fashioned in pottery, exact down to the last feather, a bird bursting with pride and the joy of greeting the sun.

"Where did you get him?" she asked, wide-eyed, as she could almost hear the bird's crowing in her ears.

Ioannis glanced over his shoulder. "Oh him! The crowing cock is sacred to the sun. It was one of the symbols of Helios. Don't you like him?"

"A very superior bird," Eleanor observed.

He grinned at her. "What did you expect?"

She dropped her eyes to her hands, aware again of that curious flutter in her middle. It had to be hunger, she thought. Goodness knows, it was long enough since she had a square meal!

"He reminds me of someone," she said at last, still not looking at him.

Ioannis merely shrugged. "Perhaps he has something to crow about," he pointed out.

"No doubt he thinks so!" she retorted. "I wonder why hens don't crow?"

His look was sardonic, making her flush. "I wonder! I should think it is because for females the chase ends in surrender and not in triumph—"

"Sometimes it does!"

"A different kind of triumph. How can the joys of surrender be the same as those of conquest. Not even the cock crows in defeat."

Eleanor sat up very straight, marvelling that she should have been fool enough to have embarked on such a conversation with him. "Surrender is not always the same thing as defeat," she said primly.

He threw the squid he had been chopping into some batter and transferred the pieces into the piping hot fat he had in a pan over the fire. Satisfied, he came back to the table and to her.

"Do you speak from personal experience, or from instinct?" he asked her.

It was absurd to be embarrassed by such a question, yet she found it curiously difficult to answer.

"Both—I think," she said.

His eyes narrowed and the look he gave her robbed her of both her confidence and her usual common sense. She didn't like being so vulnerable to his good opinion of her. What did it matter what he thought? He was a stranger to her—and likely to remain so, because she wasn't going to stay in Rhodes a day longer than she could help no matter what difficulties were put in her way!

"You're prettier than I thought you would be," he said at last. "I suppose you had all the local boys running after you?"

"Don't be ridiculous! I'm not in the least bit pretty!" she denied. "And, as for the other, why not? I'm not a candidate for a nunnery!"

He turned away, giving the pan of squid a good shake. "I find you pretty and I daresay they did too. You have no reason to sound so injured. I didn't ask if any of them caught you—"

"I'm sure you would have if you'd thought of it!" she flashed back at him, her indignation mounting by the moment.

"There was no need," he answered. "I had already received assurances on that point. You would not be here if I hadn't."

"Indeed! I've never heard anything like it! Who dared to discuss me in such terms with *you*—a man I'd never even met—"

He was quite unmoved. "Your grandmother for one. Is she forbidden to take an interest in the future of her own granddaughter?"

"Of course not! But she knows nothing about me! I hardly know her. My mother always goes to see her by herself because my father doesn't care for her much. Her English is very strange, you see, and he can never understand what she's trying to say."

"But your mother does?"

Eleanor nodded. "She speaks Greek," she explained, "but nobody else in the family does. Come to think of it, the old dear must have been rather lonely since my grandfather died." Her concern showed clearly on her face. "I wish I'd thought about it before," she said, chewing on her lip. "She could have come with me to Rhodes. It would have been like coming home to her!"

"She'll come when she's ready," Ioannis replied without much interest. "She wanted you to see the place by yourself first. She was afraid of influencing you too much in the beginning. I don't think it occurred to her that you would be lonely here on your own."

Eleanor made no attempt to hide her surprise. "She's coming *here?*"

"She will want to see for herself that the agreement has made you happy. Her brother had the idea in the first place and wrote to her about it. She had been in England a long time then and your mother told her that such arrangements went against the grain of the modern English mind—"

"What arrangements?" Eleanor asked faintly.

"I think she had better tell you that for herself," Ioannis answered. "She will be here soon enough to answer all your questions. And in the meantime we can use the time to get to know one another, *ne?*"

She would have liked to have questioned him further, but she suspected that once he had made up his mind about something it would be very difficult to shift him. She had never been backward in trying to get her own way with a man. Yet there was something about Ioannis that spelt danger to her. It would be easier and a great deal more comfortable to accept his dictums for the time being until she was more sure of her ground. And, besides, she reasoned to herself, he might not feed her otherwise. With the sight and smell of the food all round her she was hungry enough for that to be her first priority at the moment.

She watched with interest as he made the salad, tearing the lettuce into a bowl and adding a few slices of the giant-sized tomatoes, some onion, some strips of green peppers, and topping the lot with a slab of the *feta* cheese, white and damp and completely delicious.

She licked her lips expectantly as a plate was placed before her and the fried rings of squid and the potatoes were slid onto it. Silently, Ioannis handed her a fork, pushing the salt and pepper closer to her elbow.

"Bread?" he asked her.

It seemed greedy to accept but she couldn't help herself. She stuck her fork into a piece of squid and put it nervously into her mouth. It tasted sublime.

"You're a fantastic cook!" she congratulated him.

"I'm glad you think so," he smiled. "It's easy enough once you get the hang of it. You'll manage, I promise you. All you need to know is how to get the fire to work with you—and there you are!"

"There I'm not! I'll never learn to manage without an oven and proper burners that one can control. I don't even want to!"

He was amused. "Didn't you want to when you started to feel hungry?"

"In a way. Mostly I thought how nice it would be when I could leave." She looked at him uncertainly. "Aren't you having any?"

He reached up for the yellow bottle of lemon juice that was on sale all over the island and liberally doused the salad with it. "I'll share yours," he said, and proceeded to suit his action to his words by picking up a fork and helping himself to some of the food from her plate. He was completely unself-conscious about it and, belatedly, she realised he saw nothing out of the way in their sharing the food he had prepared in such intimate circumstances. Indeed, once she had got used to the idea she rather liked it herself. It added a convivial note to the proceedings.

"You know," she said, doing battle for a particular piece of squid and pleased with herself for coming off best, "I don't think my great-uncle could have understood my grandmother very well. It was just chance that it happened to be me who came out here to sell the house."

He won the next battle between their forks and then disarmed her by offering the titbit to her. He slapped his thigh. "I knew I'd forgotten something!" he exclaimed. "What we need is a glass of wine!"

She accepted that also from his hand, feeling more than a little wicked as she did so. Drinking wine in the middle of the afternoon was something she had never done before.

"I was saying," she went on, "it was just chance that I came to Rhodes. I was between jobs, you see, otherwise my mother would have come." Her forehead creased into a frown. "I don't really think my grandmother had anything to do with it at all!"

"No? The old man was her brother—"

"Yes, but they hadn't seen each other for *ages*. He may not even have known of my existence."

Ioannis offered another choice piece of squid from his fork. "Oh, he knew all about you, *koritsi mou!*" he assured her. "He made it his business to know! How you did at school and who your friends are—everything!"

Eleanor thought about that for a moment. *How could he have known?* she wondered. "My grandmother couldn't have told him all that," she said aloud. "She didn't know herself!"

"Perhaps you underrate your family's intelligence system," he suggested. "The old man certainly knew when you lost your last job. He was pleased with you for leaving when you did."

"Was he?" Eleanor said grimly. "Well, I wasn't! I should have managed it all better! The trouble is that nobody ever believes me when I say no!" It was a complaint her family had heard frequently before. "You don't sound as though you mean it," her mother had once told her. "How could you expect the poor man to know?"

Ioannis' reaction was quite different. "A girl should have someone to say no for her. Didn't your father go and see this man?"

Eleanor was horrified by the mere thought. "Good heavens, no! Why should he? I should never have allowed things to get out of hand. Only I didn't think at first he was like that." She giggled suddenly. "I prefer my octopi cooked and on a plate!"

"So you left?"

"Yes," Eleanor sighed. "It wasn't much of a job, I suppose, but it was better than nothing. And then Uncle Kostas died and I was landed with this. That's what I meant when I said it was just chance that it was I who came out here."

Ioannis transferred a piece of tomato to his own mouth. "Is that what they told you? It would have been kinder if your mother had told you more, but perhaps she was already having enough trouble with your father. I am told he is not very sympathetic to Greek ideas and manners?"

He certainly wouldn't have approved of them both eating off the same plate, Eleanor thought with relish, picturing her father's distaste for such a scene.

"It depends," Eleanor began half-heartedly. "None of us need or want a house in Rhodes!" she added. "Whatever you say, I'm going to sell it!"

He picked up a chip in his fingers and she couldn't help thinking what nice, white teeth he had. She liked the strong column of his throat too, and the way his hair curled on the back of his neck. His whole body had a healthy glow to it, and he was very strong. Even his fingers had a tough look to them, though she imagined they could be sensitive too at times. She caught herself imagining them against her own skin and she made a desperate effort to restore order to her thoughts.

"Uncle Kostas—" She rushed into speech again.

"You have no authority to sell the house," Ioannis interrupted her calmly. "For that you have to have my consent and, for the moment, I'm not prepared to give it. We'll talk about it when your grandmother comes."

Eleanor's eyes opened wide. "But what has it got to do with you?" she demanded.

"It was all in the agreement between myself and the old man," he said kindly. He leaned forward and brushed an errant hair out of her eyes and she was

23

overwhelmingly conscious of his own, closer to her than they had any right to be, two orbs of grey-green that attracted her like a moth to their brilliance.

"Then what has it got to do with me?" she asked with a breathlessness that would not be denied.

He shrugged. "It's the Greek way of managing these things," he said. "Be patient and your grandmother will explain it to you. The old man knew what he was doing, though I had my doubts at one time. Now I've seen you, however, I'm well content to let things stand. And so I can't allow you to sell the house, certainly not this afternoon!" And he leaned forward and touched his lips very gently to hers. "Are you feeling better now you've eaten?" he added on a note of laughter.

"I'd feel better still if I didn't have to spend another night in that house! It's full of shadows and peculiar noises—"

His laughter made her blink. "It's as well you have someone else to say no for you now, *koritsi mou!* But I can wait! Let's hope your grandmother arrives soon. Shall we drink to that—and to the future?"

She raised her glass to his and found herself looking at the crowing cock over his shoulder. And despite the heat of the day and the warmth from the fire and the food she had eaten, she shivered and was suddenly afraid. She swallowed down the wine hastily and very nearly choked.

"I don't believe you can stop me selling the house!" she declared violently, more than a little put out.

"No? We shall see," he said.

Chapter Two

Eleanor sat by the edge of the bright blue water, nursing her sense of grievance. The estate agent had come and gone. He had barely even glanced at her. Ioannis had made all the explanations in Greek, so she couldn't understand a word of what he was saying. The agent had looked at her briefly at first with mild interest before allowing his eyes to slide over her in an appraising, masculine stare.

Now she was wearing the briefest bikini she had brought with her. Once it had belonged to her younger sister, on whose slighter frame it had commanded little attention.

She sighed. Where was Ioannis now? He had shown no signs of caring at all when she had offered him a few home truths on the subject of the estate agent.

"I prefer that you shouldn't be leered at by strange men," he had answered coolly. "Some of our people have strange ideas about women tourists who come here—sometimes justified and sometimes not. I should prefer that you are not classed amongst those who have looser morals than we are accustomed to here."

"Indeed?" she had shouted back at him. "Well, go ahead and prefer all you like! I shall behave exactly as I choose!"

"Of course." And he had actually dared to smile at her. "As long as you choose the way I would have you choose!"

Hence the bikini. Only, she could have wished it were more comfortable to wear and, as she had been completely alone on the beach for nearly an hour now, it had rather lost its point as a gesture of defiance. She looked longingly at the terry beach dress beside her, but resisted the temptation to don it. Her sense of grievance had not subsided sufficiently for her to give in yet—and it would be giving in, she decided crossly. It was time that Ioannis learned that the average English girl was a very different cup of tea compared to the meek, submissive females he was apparently accustomed to having around him.

The sun was hot and the dampness from the sea had made her hair curl up tightly all over her head. Pretty, he had called her, but Eleanor was well aware that she was not. Her sister was the pretty one of the family, with her pale colouring and her long blonde hair. Eleanor was merely passable, having a good complexion and an immoderate zest for living that some people, mistaking enthusiasm for beauty, had made much of, though thanks to her mother, very seldom in her presence.

Now Ioannis was not exactly handsome either. Eleanor lay back on the spiky grass that was winning the battle with the grubby sand of the beach and closed her eyes, considering the man who had so unexpectedly come to torment her. No, he was not handsome, but there was something about him that threatened to overwhelm her grasp on her independence as a person. It seemed quite the natural thing to allow him to take command of her existence while she remained on Rhodes, just as it had seemed the only possible thing to allow him to feed her because she was hungry.

She could hardly believe her grandmother was coming to Rhodes. She tried to remember all she knew about her mother's Greek mother. She remembered her only as a stiff-backed, black-clad woman of an indeterminate age who had told her strange tales of a childhood on an island that at that time had been Italian and where both her religion and language had been suppressed in favour of a foreign tongue and culture they had all hated with that ruthlessness that is peculiarly Greek.

"Was it better under the Turks?" Eleanor had asked her, a little frightened by the fierce tones of this small, walnut-wrinkled woman, whose English was at best idiosyncratic and at worst completely incomprehensible.

"It is best to be free!" her grandmother had told her.

"But you never were free," Eleanor felt called upon to point out to her. "You married Grandpa and came to England."

"That was my freedom," her grandmother had answered. "Love *is* freedom. We Greeks have always understood that very well. I loved your grandfather as soon as I saw him, and nothing else mattered to me. I found freedom loving him. One day you will find it too."

"Will I?" Eleanor had been rather doubtful on that point. Living with someone like her autocratic, military-minded grandfather had not been her idea of freedom.

"If I have anything to do with it," her grandmother had responded. "I should be happy in the evening of my days to go home to Greece and, who knows, you may be there too?"

Eleanor had laughed at the thought. But she was not laughing now. It was a long, long time since she had thought about her grandmother, and longer still since she had thought about her strange ideas of freedom. Still, it explained a lot. She could imagine that her grandmother might have shared her own odd ideas with her brother, but what she couldn't believe was that they would have included her in their plans for the future, and what was even more incredible was that Ioannis might have been included also.

So intent was she on her thoughts that she didn't hear

his approach as Ioannis came down the steps that led down onto the beach from their two houses.

"I am glad to see your enforced starvation of the last few days has not affected your looks," he remarked, handing her her short terry robe.

She opened her eyes wide, an angry flush reaching up to her hair line. "I'm used to having the beach to myself," she sniffed.

"And you were lonely," he reminded her, deliberately mocking her. "Aren't you glad that now you must share it with me?"

She put on her robe with a flounce. "I see small cause for joy in that!"

"You will," he assured her. "The swimming is good from here and now that I am here you can do more than sit on the beach and look out to sea—but, not in that suit, I'm thinking. Do you have another? Or must we buy you one the next time we go into Rhodes?"

She mumbled that she didn't like swimming, that she had no intention of ever going swimming with him, and that, yes, she had two other swimming suits with her but that she doubted he would like either of them any better than the one she had on.

"Ah, but I like this one far too well!" He eyed her, his eyes as bright as the sun on the sea.

She held the flaps of her robe closely to her. "Why don't you go swimming by yourself?" she demanded. She almost added that with any luck he might drown, but suddenly, passionately, she knew she would hate it if he did. She had been alone far too much in the last few days and even his irritating company was better than none at all.

"It's the wind that whips up the waves," he told her. "There is very little current in this bay. Go and change your suit, Eleanor. You'll be quite safe with me!"

She wanted badly to defy him. It shone out of her eyes and showed in her outraged stance as she twisted the wooden buttons of her coat in an agony of indecision. And, on top of everything else, he had not been shocked at all, merely amused by her. It was that which decided her. She went up the steps to the house without a word, her eyes pricking with unshed tears. He was so—so sure of himself!

She buried the offending bikini at the bottom of the chest that held her clothes, choosing the newer of her two other suits, a garment that wouldn't have raised an eyebrow anywhere in the world. It was black and it suited her but, looking at herself in the glass, it quite failed to please her. Her body looked white and cold against his smooth, golden tan, and she wished she had spent longer out in the sun before he had come, but the beach had bored her and she had been afraid to risk swimming out very far when she had been alone.

She decided against going back to the beach empty-handed. She had acquired a taste for the local lemonade in the last few days and she took a couple of bottles with her now, opening them with a flick of her wrist and dropping a straw into each of them. She flung herself down on the ground beside him and handed him one of the bottles.

"Peace?" she said, her long eyelashes veiling her look.

"Of course, peace," he agreed at once. He poured a very small quantity of the lemonade onto the sand between them. "A libation to Helios and his all-seeing eye. Now neither of us will dare to break the pact, *ne?*"

"I hope he is a forgiving god," she said doubtfully.

Ioannis smiled slowly. "Have you so little faith in your own good intentions?" he quizzed her.

"Not in mine!" she denied. "My intentions are always good!"

He ran his fingers down her arm to her hand, enclosing it in his own. "You suit Rhodes very well, after all. You share her swift changes of mood and the unexpected vistas of beauty—"

She wrenched her hand away from his. "What nonsense you do talk!" she chided him. "None of the gods really existed, so how can we possibly know how they felt? They're—they're just stories."

He shrugged. "They are very, very old stories and wouldn't have survived down the ages unless they somehow fitted the human heart. Mock them at your peril, Eleanor mine!"

She winced. "I am not yours!"

He turned his eyes fully onto her face. "Not yet," he said.

Her face burned as scarlet as if she had been touched by the sun. "I wish you wouldn't!" she murmured. She avoided his eyes and swallowed down the last of her lemonade. "Ioannis, I don't think like my grandmother. I may have some of her blood in my veins, but it's been completely swamped by the English side. Uncle Kostas and Grandma may have made some kind of an agreement with you, but I didn't, and I won't ever! I'm not Greek enough for that, you see!"

He turned over on his stomach, smiling up at her. "Bravely said!" he commended her. "I like it that you are English and cool. But you are also a woman, albeit an Englishwoman, and you have yet to discover what you think about that. Be still, Eleanor, and wait for your grandmother to come. We shall see then what the future holds."

Her moment of courage deserted her. Her grandmother would have to explain it to him, she decided. It would serve her right for having cooked up such a ludicrous notion in the first place!

"We don't do things like that in England!" Eleanor said aloud, pursing her mouth up tight in disapproval. "We make up our own minds whom we want to marry!"

He brushed the sand from her fingers and her flesh tingled pleasantly under his touch. "Do you imagine we don't in Greece? The only difference is that here the girl has someone to protect her interests and to say no on her behalf. With women the urge to please is very strong and it is hard for her to separate the unscrupulous from the determined. I think ours is the better way!"

She gave him a disgruntled look. "Women aren't necessarily fools, you know!"

He linked his fingers around her wrist. "But easier to seduce than the more objective male," he suggested. "Do you think I couldn't persuade you to my way of thinking?"

"I know you couldn't!" But she wasn't quite so sure inside. She was very much aware of his light grasp. In fact she could think of nothing else—that and the firmness of his skin, and his light green eyes in which all common sense could drown if she were not very careful.

His breath fanned her cheek and she averted her face hastily, but not before he had felt her slight shiver of anticipation and had brushed his lips against hers in a second kiss that was quite as unsatisfactory as the first.

He leaped to his feet, his hand still on her wrist. "Come on, *yinéka mou,* we are going swimming before we both get carried away—"

"It isn't very objective to get carried away with someone I've just met!" she tore out scornfully.

His eyebrows rose. "You are more vulnerable than you think! But we shall wait for your grandmother to come all the same!"

Her eyes fell before his. "She'll tell you that I had no part in any arrangement you made with my uncle! I want to go back to England!"

His lips twitched. "I thought you also wanted to see my *caique?*"

Defeated, she nodded her head. "I want that too," she admitted. "But that has nothing to do with the other, has it?"

His expression was kind, almost affectionate. "Today has nothing to do with any other day," he compromised. "Today, there are no problems that either of us need worry about. Okay?"

She nodded again, unaccountably relieved. "Suits me," she said. "Anyway, there isn't any problem because I won't let there be. I never heard anything so ridiculous in my life! You can't force me into something like that against my will!"

33

His smile demolished her new confidence with an ease that rendered her breathless. "Not if it *is* against your will," he said.

It was indeed an evening caught up out of time. Eleanor had never experienced anything like it before and she enjoyed every moment of it with an intensity that amused her faintly blasé host, a fact which he didn't trouble to conceal from her.

Ioannis wouldn't permit her to swim out to the *caique* in the end. It was too far for someone who swam as seldom as she did, he decided. He would swim out by himself and would return with the tender to collect her and the clothes they would need that evening.

"Clothes?" she said blankly. "What clothes?"

"Haven't you a pretty dress with you?"

"Of course!"

"Then go and fetch it," he bade her. "And anything else you might need for an evening out on the town. And, while you're about it, bring my clothes too, will you? You'll find them on the chair beneath the *sophas*."

The word was still strange to her. "*Sophas?*" she repeated.

"The platform that serves as a bed," he reminded her with deliberate mockery. "You needn't go up there unless you wish!"

She jerked her head upwards, annoyed that he had succeeded in embarrassing her.

"I find it difficult enough to climb up to my own bed," she said, "without making an unnecessary trip up to yours!"

His lips curved into a smile. "One day—"

"It's an uncivilised arrangement!" She cut him off. "I hate sleeping on the floor at the best of times, and with that stifling curtain all round one, I hate it still more!"

"The curtain keeps the mosquitos away," he said solemnly. "You would be bitten alive without it."

"No, I wouldn't. I have some insect repellent with me. I got it in England before I came—"

"Then it must be good!"

She suspected he was teasing her and a reluctant smile broke across his face. "Well, wouldn't you prefer a proper bed?" she demanded.

"I'm accustomed to sleeping in strange places," he answered.

She looked down her nose. "Now that I can easily believe," she murmured.

He took a step towards her and she knew an instant of pure fear as he faced up to her. "Eleanor, go and fetch the clothes, there's a good girl!" He turned away from her, throwing over his shoulder as he went, "And keep that imagination of yours in check, *agapí*. It doesn't suit you when you put that disapproving look on your face!"

"I never said I disapproved!" she denied hotly.

"Then you should!" he retorted.

He was gone by the time she could gather her scattered wits. She watched him walk out into the royal blue water, striking out strongly for the distant boat. She could never have kept up with him, she admitted reluctantly to herself. She could swim quite well, but he was in a quite different class from her own modest efforts. It was a joy to watch him, cutting cleanly through the foam-topped waves.

She wondered again what it would be like to be loved by him—and as quickly backed away from her own thoughts again, running up the steps to their two houses as though the devil himself was after her.

Her own clothes were easily found and put in a plastic bag, ready for when she would need them. His clothes took her much longer to get. They were on the chair, exactly where he had said they would be, a pair of pale green Levis and a cheesecloth shirt embroidered in blue with the double-headed eagle of Greece. She rolled them up and put them in the bag with her own, adding a pair of shoes and his clean underclothes. It was only after she had pushed them away out of sight that she was tempted to take a good look round his house and see how it differed from her own next door.

The crowing cock she ignored. She felt slightly uncomfortable whenever she looked at it, almost as if it were jeering at her and something inside her knew why, only she didn't care to recognise that particular piece of knowledge. Only the cock knew that she knew. She could go on hiding it from herself forever and, if she could do that, she could hide it just as easily from Ioannis!

Hyperion!

If it were true that the sun had an all-seeing eye, perhaps she wouldn't be able to hide it from him for long. Not that it mattered. It *couldn't* matter. She wasn't the first girl whose eye had been pleased by a strong, masculine body and a pair of light, green-grey eyes.

The clothes chest, opposite the platform that held his bedding, was very old and intricately carved. She wouldn't let herself look at the steps that led up to the *sophas* at first and, when she did so, she saw they were old and worn and probably creaked as badly as did her own.

Ioannis had already rowed back to the beach when she sauntered down the steps to rejoin him. He helped her into the tender, his fingers warm against hers, and dropped the plastic bag onto her knee.

"I hope you're feeling hungry again?" he said to her.

"Not yet. But I'm going to be in a moment," she assured him. "I have several days of semi-starvation to make up." She sighed. "My sister is an excellent cook. *She* wouldn't have let a sulky fire defeat her if she had wanted a meal. It's a pity my family didn't think of that before they sent me to cope with Uncle Kostas' house!"

"Is your sister older than you?"

Eleanor shook her head. "She's two years younger, but she's much better able to cope in an emergency than I am," she said. "She doesn't mind saying no, you see. In fact sometimes she takes an active pleasure in it!" She sounded half-envious, half-admiring of her sister's strength of mind, and more than a little impatient with herself. "She said no firmly enough when it was suggested that she would be the better person sent out here. I said no too, but nobody bothered to listen, and I've already made a mess of things, allowing you to send the land agent away like that!"

Ioannis looked at her, rowing in silence while he did so. "It was always intended that you should come," he said at last. "Your sister wouldn't have done at all."

Eleanor didn't like to ask him what he meant by that.

She tried to escape the fascination of his eyes by looking at the approaching *caique* over her shoulder. It was bigger than it had looked from the shore, with a wooden hull, a high prow, and neatly furled rust-red sails.

"She's beautiful!" she said under her breath. "But can you manage to sail her single-handed? She looks awfully big!"

"I'll have you to help me," he reminded her. But, when it came to it, she wasn't much use to him, though she liked it very much when he put the tiller into her hands. She could feel the boat straining beneath her, like a living thing that was glorying in the exultant chase before the fresh wind.

Rhodes harbour came far too quickly. The sun was just setting as they drifted between the two pillars that marked the legendary site where the gigantic Colossus of Rhodes had once stood, the ships coming and going between his bronze thighs. Beyond them were three drum-shaped, stone windmills, built during the Middle Ages to mill the grain for departing cargo boats. Their jib-like sails flapped gently in the breeze and then they were hidden from view by a forest of masts of other boats moored along the quay of the harbour.

They took turns changing in the cabin down below and then Ioannis walked her into the old town, passing through the fortified gateway that had once helped defend the last of the Crusaders of Europe. Despite the lateness of the hour, the narrow, cobbled streets were full of life. The shops had not yet shut and the restaurants were already open.

Ioannis chose a table out on the street where they

were served with *soúpa avgolémono,* made fi
chicken stock, eggs and rice, and flavoured with lemon
juice, followed by lobster, locally caught, and served
with a Greek salad on the side. As it grew darker a
group of traditionally dressed singers came and sang
some of the *syrtaki* and some of the men diners rose
and danced with a mournful intensity that was oddly
moving.

Eleanor could have gone on sitting there all night,
but shortly after eleven o'clock Ioannis insisted they
should leave. He paid the bill with a flourish. Although
she thought she ought to have volunteered her share,
she knew he would never accept that, so she contented
herself with thanking him warmly for the evening,
determined to stay awake long enough to be more of a
help to him in sailing the *caique* home than she had
been on the way out.

The sea looked remote and mysterious in the moonlight. She dabbled her fingers in their wake as he rowed
the tender back to the shore. He helped her out onto
the beach, putting his hands under her arms and lifting
her high over the water's edge to avoid soaking her
pretty evening sandals.

"You should sleep well tonight," he laughed down at
her, without releasing her. "You're half asleep now!"

"I've enjoyed myself," she answered. "I wish I could
sleep out here instead of on that stuffy shelf."

He turned her face up to his, and he was still smiling.
"Tonight there will be nothing to frighten you," he
assured her. "You have only to remember that I'm next
door and you won't hear another sound."

She made a slight movement towards him, more

39

grateful for his presence than she could say, and he caught her up against him and kissed her soundly, his lips firm and tasting of salt against hers.

"Eleanor!"

She blinked into the darkness and, belatedly, recognised the small, upright figure standing on the stone steps above them.

"Grandma," she said weakly. And then again. *"Grandma!"*

Chapter Three

"We will talk about it in the morning," Mrs. Barron said in sufficiently quelling tones to make Eleanor hope the morning never came. "It is late and I am tired."

"But, Grandma, it wasn't like that!" Eleanor was moved to protest.

Her grandmother said something in Greek, her meaning sufficiently obvious to raise Eleanor's colour and temper in equal proportion. "Of course it was like that!" the older woman went on in English, her accent making her sound more foreign than any relative, especially such a close one, ever ought to be. "You had far better keep silent, Eleanor, until you have thought out exactly what it is you wish to say. It will suffice now to tell you I am not entirely displeased—though such behaviour is not what I would expect from a *Greek* girl!"

Eleanor quelled the impulse to tell her that she was not Greek, never would be Greek, and had no ambition even to emulate anything that was Greek.

"I happen to be English," she said dryly, "and we exchange kisses with our escorts all the time, Grandma dear, and it doesn't mean a thing!"

"Which is why you gave up your last job, I suppose?" her grandmother retorted. "Go to bed, Eleanor, and try to grow up a little bit before we discuss this again in the morning."

Eleanor could have stamped her foot with rage. Somehow or other, her grandmother had succeeded in making her feel guilty. Yet it wasn't as though she had intended to let Ioannis kiss her. It had taken her completely by surprise, or at least she thought it had been like that. It was true she hadn't raised any objection, for it had seemed the most natural thing in the world. She felt again the heat of his lips against hers and the wild sensation of excitement that had overtaken her, and she felt guiltier than ever. Her bewilderment was reflected in her eyes and the look on her face.

"I'd better make up a bed for you," she said in shaken tones. "In fact you'd better have my bed and I'll move into the other room. I don't think the bedding is very well aired and your rheumatism—"

"That is kind of you, my dear. Especially as the

timing of my arrival seems to have upset you so much. Did you have any other plans for the evening?"

Eleanor could only stare at her. "Of course not!"

Her grandmother's face softened. "My dear, I'm not questioning your morals, only the strength of your resistance to that extremely attractive young man next door."

"That's too much!" Eleanor exploded, finally losing her temper. "My resistance is splendid, thank you! If you'd wanted it to be otherwise you should have sent Sonia to Rhodes in my place. She would have soon told you what you could do with the arrangement you seem to have made with Uncle Kostas—"

Her grandmother laughed softly. "It never occurred to me to give your sister such an opportunity. It would be quite lost on her. She has none of your gift for what I believe is called serendipity. It quite simply wouldn't have worked!"

"Serendipity?" Eleanor repeated cautiously. "What is that?"

"The gift of being surprised by joy at the most unexpected things. The Arabs called Ceylon, or Sri Lanka, or whatever it is called now, Serendip, because round every corner they came across a new beauty to delight them. I suppose serendipity comes from that."

Eleanor's eyes widened with surprise. "Wherever did you hear that?"

"I read," Mrs. Barron answered. "I understand English very well, as I should by now. There is no accent to confuse one on paper either. Don't be misled by mine, *kora mou*. I understand you too, better than you think!"

Eleanor could only hope she was wrong about that! She couldn't understand herself at all!

"Why don't you think Sonia has serendipity?" she asked as she went across to the *pangos*, the chest that held clothing and extra bedding and the other household effects that were better stowed away when they were not in use.

"She is far too decided a young lady to be surprised by anything," Mrs. Barron answered.

"Lucky thing!" Eleanor said with a viciousness that brought a mocking, faintly malicious look to her grandmother's face.

"Do you think so? I should rather be truly loved by someone who was going to make most of my decisions for me." She sighed. "How I miss your grandfather for that! I hate having to decide for myself what I am going to do."

"But—"

"He really cared that he should do the best thing for me, you see," her grandmother went on. "He would worry if he thought I was working too hard, or if the children were too much for me, or if I looked pale from living in the city too long. Now there is no one to care what I do with myself."

"Oh, Grandma! We all care!" She bit her lip, aware that that was not the whole truth. Of course they cared when they thought about her, but they had often been impatient with her too. "I'm sorry, Grandma," she murmured uncomfortably. "Perhaps we haven't cared enough, but we don't see you very often, do we?"

"I believe that you care," Mrs. Barron agreed gently. "You are soft-hearted enough to care what happens even to those you despise, as your sister despises me for being foreign and having a quaint accent!" She held up her hand when Eleanor started to defend Sonia. *"You* care, Eleanor, but you can never make up your mind what to do for the best for yourself."

"Oh, Grandma!" Eleanor reproached her. "I'm not quite as feeble as all that!"

"I wouldn't have described it as being *feeble,"* Mrs. Barron denied, suppressing a smile. "Does it matter that you prefer to cooperate with someone else's ideas than make the initiative yourself? I do myself, and I have never thought of myself as being particularly feeble!"

Eleanor gathered up the bedding to her and turned and faced her grandmother. "But I want to be independent and make my own decisions. Only, I get all muddled up, especially when it comes to other people. How can one be sure that one really knows what is best for them? Sonia thinks she knows—"

Her grandmother chuckled. "Did she advise you to stick it out with that last employer of yours? Don't be a ninny, Eleanor"—she did an excellent imitation of her younger granddaughter—"the job is well-paid, and you won't get another one like it in a hurry. Make the most of things as they are!"

"She might have been right," Eleanor pointed out. "If it had been she, she would have had everything under control right from the beginning!"

"And you find that admirable?"

Not only admirable, Eleanor thought with feeling, she was downright envious of her sister's ability to cope with the opposite sex in any emergency.

"Don't you?" she said lightly.

"Sometimes. Indecision can be a kind of encouragement to some men. Was it that that made young Nikkolides think he could kiss you with impunity?"

Eleanor's breath caught in the back of her throat. "*No!* No, I don't think so. It was only because he'd taken me out to dinner and it was the most beautiful evening! The music—and the dancing, even though it was only the men who danced. He said I wasn't to, that I'd be taken for a tourist if I tried to dance in a restaurant—"

"And you agreed with that?"

Eleanor shrugged. "He knows the local customs better than I do."

"I doubt that would have stopped Sonia," Mrs. Barron said dryly. Her eyes rested on her granddaughter's flushed face. "However, he was quite right. Traditionally, men have always danced in the restaurants and women in the squares and other open spaces. It was a good thing you had him with you to prevent you from making a fool of yourself!"

Eleanor made no answer to that. She hugged the bedding closer to her and rushed out into the courtyard without a backward glance, struggling with the door of the secondary and slightly smaller room that refused to give way to her agitated fingers.

"Goodnight, little Eleanor," Ioannis' voice came over the wall to her, and then, a couple of seconds later, "Can I help?"

"I can't open the door!" she whispered, scared her grandmother would hear her and catch her with Ioannis again.

46

"Have you tried using the key?" he suggested, her struggles beginning to amuse him.

"How can I?" she demanded. "What do you suggest I do with all this bedding?"

He came and joined her in the courtyard, opening the door for her with a flick of his wrist. He stood back to let her go past him, a wicked smile on his face. "Is there anything else I can do for you while I'm here?" he asked, *sotto voce*.

"Nothing!" she answered grandly, doing her best not to trip over the trailing sheets. "Nothing at all!"

He took the bedding from her, pushing her out of his way as he strode over to the platform at the far end. He mounted the steps with an ease that was quite unlike her own fumbling approach to them, and spread the bedding neatly out onto the mattress he found there.

"If you can brave your grandmother again, I'd suggest you go back for a pillow," he said over his shoulder.

Eleanor stood in the middle of the room, her face mutinous. "I'm not afraid of her! I'm not afraid of anyone!" she declared, and as promptly wished she had said something a little less silly. "She doesn't understand, that's all," she added defensively.

"My kissing you?"

She shook her head. "My allowing you to!"

He sat on the top of the steps and looked at her. "Did you allow me to?" he asked, much interested. "To tell the truth, I had thought it my idea and that you had very little say in the matter."

"Oh," she said, feeling more foolish than ever. The colour burned a passage up her throat and face as she remembered that far from giving any impression that she had been unwilling to be kissed, she had actually made a small, impulsive movement towards him that he could hardly have helped but notice. He was not, after all, an unobservant man. "Well, however it was," she went on in a choking voice, "Grandma says no *Greek* girl would have permitted such a liberty, though I can't believe they're so different from us!"

"My sweet girl, in Greece it is always the man's fault. Didn't your grandmother tell you that while she was about it?"

Eleanor twisted her fingers together. "Perhaps, in Greece, it *is* always the man's fault." she suggested on a stubborn note.

"Perhaps it is," he agreed, far too readily for her liking. "Like most men, they prefer to be the huntsmen rather than the quarry."

"The *quarry!* I may not be decisive, but at least I know enough not to want to be any man's quarry, thank you very much!" She pursed her lips. "Whatever next?" she demanded.

He cupped her chin on his hands. "I could kiss you again," he said with an impudence that took her breath away.

"N-not here!"

He laughed, throwing back his head and letting out a volume of sound that made her want to cover her ears and go running back to her grandmother. Yet she was a little bit curious too, wondering if he really would dare to kiss her again in the face of her grandmother's expressed disapproval. She took a look at him from under her lashes and looked as hastily away again, deeply conscious of the sudden tensing of his muscles and the look of naked invitation on his face.

"Somewhere else?" he said on a suggestive note.

"Certainly not!" That had sounded decisive enough to have been her sister speaking. "Besides, where else is there?" she added, completely ruining her effect. She bit her lip, mortified. "I wish you'd go away!"

He stood up, looking unbelievably tall at the top of three or four steps that led up to the *sophas*. "Another place, another time," he murmured, and came down the stairs towards her.

She cowered back. "Haven't you done enough harm already?" she demanded.

He paused beside her, turning her face up to his with his fingers under her chin. "Running scared, little Eleanor? Who are you afraid of, I wonder, me or yourself?"

She swallowed, wishing she had the strength of mind to wrench herself free of him, or even to call out to her grandmother in the other room. While she was still hesitating, he put his lips against hers in a kiss as soft as thistledown, and was gone out of the door.

Somewhere outside, with a blithe disregard that it was the middle of the night and that sunrise was still several hours away, a cock crowed. As far as Eleanor was concerned it was the last straw. She took a run headlong up the steep steps to her bed and wept bitter tears of defeat until she could cry no more. It was only then she realised she was still without a pillow and that it was too late to disturb her grandmother again. And at that moment, the cock took it into his head to crow again and the mocking note resounded in her ears until she could have wrung his neck. On which blood-thirsty note she finally fell asleep.

The cock was still at it when she woke. For a long moment she wondered why she was fully dressed and had a crick in her neck, but memory slowly seeped back to her and she clenched her fists against the recollection of Ioannis' caress and the note of triumph on which he had shut the door after his departure.

Who needed serendipity at such a time, she asked herself. Serendipity indeed! But she couldn't quite shut out the recollection that there had been more than a touch of joy in the feel of Ioannis' lips on hers. It was the merest physical attraction of course, compounded of clean-cut, warm, tanned flesh that smelt of the sun and the sea and an outdoor, male life that had never come her way before. It couldn't mean anything more than that for there was nothing for her here in Rhodes. She had known that as soon as she had seen the house. She simply wasn't cut out for the primitive life, though it was funny how far away and dull London could seem first thing in the morning.

Her grandmother was already up and dressed when Eleanor went out into the courtyard, yawning and stretching to ease the knots in the muscles of her back.

"Good morning, dear," Mrs. Barron greeted her. "Feeling like breakfast yet?"

Eleanor smiled at her black-clad relative who seemed to be completely at home in her brother's house. "I meant to give you breakfast in bed," she said. "It's about the only meal I can manage on that fire!"

"You will soon get used to it," her grandmother consoled her. "A few lessons from me and you'll get the hang of it in no time!" Her shrewd eyes explored her granddaughter's face, noting the traces of the tears of the night before on her cheeks. "Go and wash first and then we can eat our bread and honey and drink our coffee in peace. You look in need of a lazy day! Did that foolish bird keep you awake last night?"

Eleanor looked blank. "Bird? What bird?"

Her grandmother's look was distinctly mocking. "You didn't hear Hyperion in the night, I suppose?"

Eleanor's guilty start was nothing, compared to the embarrassed confusion that suffused her face. "What makes you think he's called Hyperion?" she asked defensively.

"My dear girl, Kostas' cocks are always called Hyperion! I was quite glad to hear him crowing, as a matter of fact, as presumably where he is, the hens are also. Have you found any eggs around the place since you got here?"

"I haven't looked," Eleanor confessed. "I don't remember any cock crowing before either. If I did, I didn't connect it with hens and eggs, I'm afraid."

Her grandmother laughed, her whole body heaving up and down with mirth. She looked more Greek by the moment, Eleanor thought, standing in what could only have been a Greek yard, without any of the corsets she had always worn in England, and without a sign of any makeup on her walnut wrinkled face.

"What did you connect him with? The rising sun?"

"Not even that," Eleanor said in relief. "I didn't

know then he was sacred to Helios—in fact I'd never heard of Helios or Hyperion!"

"But you know all about him now. Did that young man tell you his legend? He looks as though he's on good terms with the sun, that one! How long has he been back?"

"He came yesterday."

Eleanor didn't want to talk about Ioannis, nor, when she came to think about it, did she want to dwell on crowing cocks and the significance the ancients had given to all such birds. Today was the day she was going to have to be very firm and win the battle she knew was going to be fought between them.

Her grandmother took one look at her granddaughter's grim expression and chuckled to herself, settling herself more comfortably in the rocking chair she had dragged out into the courtyard from the main room.

"Kostas would never allow anyone else to sit on his chair when he was alive," she confided to Eleanor. "I always wanted to, and he knew it too. But I was brought up to respect the little privileges of my menfolk and I never quite dared to defy him and sit on it anyway when I visited him. Now I can sit on it and welcome, and I find it rather sad. I'm getting sentimental in my old age!"

"You're not old, Grandma!" Eleanor protested.

"Sometimes I feel very old. I have lived the best days of my life and that makes one old. More and more, in recent years, I have wanted to return to Rhodes, to where I lived as a girl, amongst the people and things I know and understand. I should like to end my days here in this house, without having to pretend I am something I am not. Kostas knew that. He understood, because it's the way he would have felt himself. He did his best to make it all come true for me. You're not going to spoil it all for a childish whim, are you, Eleanor?"

Old age was often selfish and self-centered, Eleanor reflected uneasily, yet she couldn't ignore her grand-mother's appeal.

"If we sold this house to the hotel people there would be more than enough for you to live anywhere you chose," she said aloud. "The land agent came yester-day, but Ioannis sent him away. He said I couldn't sell without his permission. Do let's sell, Grandma! It would be by far the best thing for both of us!"

Mrs. Barron shook her head. "Kostas left the house as your *prika*. It will be for your husband to sell it, or not, as he chooses. But how much I should like to live here, in the house where I was born, and be at peace!"

"Yes, but, Grandma, you can't expect me—"

"I wouldn't, if you were unwilling—but you weren't unwilling last night! If you want the sweets of life, my dear, you have to pay the price!"

"But I told you, it meant nothing—nothing to either of us! It was just a kiss!"

Mrs. Barron sipped her coffee. "Since when was a kiss nothing, my girl? Silly child! I should have thought much less of you if you didn't occasionally allow your heart to rule your head. *That* has always been the way of us Greek women. We are hot-blooded, passionate people who need to give our whole allegiance to the one we love! Do you think I felt any less than that for your grandfather? It is only now that I am without him that I want to come home to my own people. If he were alive now, I'd cross the whole world to find him—"

"But you were married—"

Her grandmother thought poorly of such an irrelevant interruption and clicked her tongue angrily against her teeth. *"But Ioannis is not!* And that is whom we are talking about, my girl! *He* is the one Kostas and I arranged for you to marry and you find him very much to your taste, so don't pretend you don't!"

Eleanor drew herself up with dignity. "I won't be arranged into anything, Grandma! I'm telling you now, before this goes any further, that I'm saying no. N-o, *No!* I'm not going to marry anyone to please you, Uncle Kostas, or anyone else!" Her mouth trembled despite herself. "How could you think that I would? Do you think I have no pride at all?"

"Pride is a poor bedfellow," her grandmother mocked her. She leaned forward in her rocking chair and buttered a piece of still-warm fresh bread, spreading it liberally with honey and handing it to Eleanor. "Perhaps I shouldn't have allowed Kostas to persuade me you would accept our Greek ways without any preparation, but you forget that that was the way I was brought up too. Do you want to die an old maid?"

"Yes!"

The older woman's laughter made her want to cry. She knew she was being ridiculous, that she wanted to marry like everyone else and have a man to love and children of her own, but she wasn't going to be bullied into it with someone she hardly knew.

"If you mean that, you've done yourself no service

54

by encouraging that young man to think otherwise," her grandmother told her with relish. "You cooked your own goose then, my girl, without any help from me! You won't catch a young man like that thinking that any granddaughter of mine would allow herself to be kissed unless she means to have him! You can say no as often as you like to me, but he'll soon bring you to heel—and no doubt you'll love him all the more for it! You see if you don't!"

Eleanor put the uneaten bread and honey down on the table beside her grandmother and turned on her heel, going into the secondary room where she had slept the night before without another word. She dressed herself with shaking hands, running a comb through her tightly curled hair that, since coming to Rhodes, seemed to live a life of its own, refusing to be moulded into the soft waves it obliged her with at home.

"Where are you going?" Mrs. Barron asked without much interest as she reappeared in the doorway.

"Out," Eleanor answered her. "I shall be out all day!"

"Take care," her grandmother bade her. "It will do you good to be by yourself to think things over, but don't fret, girl. I wouldn't have agreed to anything Kostas said if it hadn't been the best thing for you. What kind of a man would you have found for yourself in England? Be advised by me and take Ioannis while you can and be thankful!"

Eleanor set her mouth in a firm line and answered not a word. She couldn't even bring herself to look in her grandmother's direction. She didn't know where she was going, but going she was, as far and as fast as her legs would carry her. She would catch the bus into Rhodes Town and lose herself amongst the crowds of tourists who gathered in Mandraki Harbour—and she would try not to think about the delights of the evening before, and of Ioannis she would not think at all!

Yet she couldn't help glancing through the open gate into his courtyard as she went past. He, too, was sitting out in the sunshine, a transistor radio on the table beside him on which was being broadcast the unmistakable chanting of the Greek Orthodox Mass. He crossed himself as she went by, touching his right shoulder before his left in the Orthodox manner. She had never in her whole life seen anyone do that before, not even her grandmother on her rare visits to her parents' home. And this was the man they wanted her to marry!

All the way to the bus stop, she kept telling herself that she could never grow used to the sensuous, golden quality of a church that would always be foreign to her, but the sound of the cantor, pouring out of every household as she passed, was lighting a candle in her heart, giving her a satisfaction she didn't even try to explain to herself. It was like everything else in Greece: warm, golden and vibrant.

The bus stopped for her and she bought herself a ticket, sitting down quickly on the nearest grey, slippery seat. She had much more money in her purse than she had thought, more than enough to see her through the day. She could do it in style, she thought, do anything she chose and there would be nothing and no one to stop her.

She would go on a boat trip, she decided. She would

go to Symi! The boats only went there on Sundays and Tuesdays, and that would be something else she could do. She would buy a return ticket and stay there for the two nights, a long, long way from her grandmother and Ioannis. Even they would have to understand that she meant "no" after that!

Chapter Four

Eleanor gave herself a little shake. She had run away so that she might escape from Helios, Hyperion and Ioannis, a trinity that would always be a trifle confused in her mind. They were unwanted baggage that kept turning up no matter how hard she tried to throw them overboard. She was sitting alone on one of the slatted rafts that were all that there were to sit on on the overcrowded aft deck of the small steamship that plied its way from one of the nineteen hundred Aegean islands to another all its days.

As the Turkish landscape, bleak and apparently

uninhabited, slipped past, she tried to think seriously about her grandmother. It had been a year or two since she had last seen her. It occurred to Eleanor that Mrs. Barron had never appeared at her best in her daughter's home. Mrs. Stewart had spoken to her always in Greek, thus creating an invisible barrier between her and the rest of the family. Neither Eleanor's father, nor Sonia, had made the faintest effort to understand her heavily accented English. Although Eleanor, more from good manners than out of any real feeling, had listened to her stories about her grandfather's doings, they had mostly gone in one ear and straight out the other.

Mrs. Barron had grown more silent as the visit had progressed. Once Eleanor had met her in the centre of London for lunch, a rather bitter occasion as it had been the one day when her boyfriend of the moment had been able to meet her that week. They had gone to a Cypriot restaurant, Eleanor remembered, cheap and not particularly clean, where the food had been a woeful parody of what Greek food can be. Surprisingly, the two of them had enjoyed themselves. Eleanor had been very conscious of her role as hostess and her grandmother had played the part of guest to perfection—until those last few moments when Eleanor had been fool enough to tell her about a party she had attended the week before. She wouldn't have done so if she hadn't still had it on her mind, for to tell the truth she had been rather shocked by all that had happened there.

"There was a police raid," she had burst out to her grandmother. "I managed to get out through the lavatory window—with a little help from Roland. He was in a hurry to get out himself, I expect.''

"He was in the ladies'?" her grandmother had enquired with raised eyebrows.

"Oh, everything is unisex these days!" Eleanor had assured her. "It was all rather exciting. Only"—she had hesitated, wondering why on earth she should have chosen to confide in such an unlikely person as her straight-laced grandmother—"only I think Roland was one of the people the police were after and afterwards he wouldn't go home! I can't help liking him though. I've never known anyone like him!" And she had thought, rather painfully, of the telephone call they had exchanged just before lunch when she had told him she wasn't available at lunchtime. Had he meant that there would be any number of other girls who would be, and that *they* wouldn't have her square and rigid ideas on right and wrong either?

"What do your parents think of Roland?" had been her grandmother's only comment.

Eleanor had been taken by surprise. "They've never met him! He isn't the sort of person you take home to mother, if you know what I mean?"

"I think I do," her grandmother had said.

There had been something in her voice that had told Eleanor she had made a mistake in saying one word about Roland. She had been certain of it when Mrs. Barron had gone on to say, "Don't worry about him, my dear. I hadn't realised how grown up you are nowadays and, if your parents won't do anything about it, I suppose I must. This has been a delightful luncheon—a treat I shall remember for a long, long time!"

And that had made it all worthwhile for Eleanor. She had looked on her grandmother with kindly eyes, almost loving her. "I wish it had been a really Greek meal though," she had sighed and had bubbled over with a new and even better idea. "Why don't you cook one for us at home? It would be super if you would!"

Mrs. Barron had looked down, her hooded lids hiding her thoughts. "I doubt your father would think it a super idea," was all she had said.

Eleanor had deliberately grinned at her grandmother, a slightly wicked grin that brought her whole face to life. "Don't they miss a lot?" she had said.

Now she knew exactly what a mistake it had been to tell her Greek and, let's face it, extraordinarily old-fashioned grandmother about Roland. She had probably decided to write to her brother then and there.

But understanding her grandmother's motives didn't help her one bit now that Eleanor was faced with the result. And what about Ioannis? Had *he* nothing to say about this? That was the strangest thing of all, she considered, because he wasn't the type of man who would allow anyone else, no matter who they were, to make his decisions for him. Eleanor didn't know how she knew that, but she knew it in every fibre of her being. Ioannis was his own man and, if he had decided to fall in with Uncle Kostas' plans for the disposal of his great-niece, he would have his own reasons for doing so. Only, whatever could they be? Her heart quaked within her. That was the most frightening aspect of the whole thing. *What did Ioannis want from her?* What could he want—and why?

Symi, first a shadow on the horizon, was now plainly visible. It was the most unsympathetic island Eleanor had ever seen. The most that grew on the rocky slopes that heaved themselves out of the blue-black water was some short, scrubby bushes on which nothing could have lived.

A glimpse of a harbour, followed by an endless stretch of gaunt, rocky slopes, and then the ship turned slowly into the entrance of another harbour. Symi Town lay before them in neoclassical perfection, multi-coloured, dazzling in the hot sun, the houses grouped round the long, deep harbor, rising by way of steps onto the surrounding hills.

The ship emptied her passengers onto the quay in a matter of moments. The Scandinavians clustered round their guides for the day. They walked briskly from one site to another, their cameras clicking as they went.

Eleanor, made lazy by the sun, drifted round the corner to where she had seen some thatched umbrellas guarding a few metal tables. She paused to buy herself a lemonade, then settled herself down in a patch of shade and looked about her.

A fishing boat came into the harbour, its two-stroke engine rending the silence with the persistence of an angry insect. It was followed by a *caique,* moving more slowly, the rust-brown sails flapping in the fast-dying breeze. Eleanor watched it disappear round the corner and thought no more about it. Her lemonade was deliciously cool and her mind was a blessed blank.

"Hullo, Eleanor."

The back of her neck prickled in alarm and she dropped the book out of her hand. She shut her eyes and refused to answer. How could she have seen those rust-red sails and not have known whose *caique* it was? Yet what could she have done if she had known? She could hardly have leaped into the sea!

She opened her eyes again. "What are you doing here?"

Ioannis sat down on the chair opposite her, his legs stretched out in front of him, looking the picture of ease. "Shall I go away again?" he asked her.

She shook her head. She had been lonely long enough. Besides, if he stayed she could explain to him why her grandmother had acted in the way she had. He could hardly blame her for the resulting muddle. He might even tell her why he had agreed to Uncle Kostas' outrageous proposal in the first place. If he hadn't, this silly misunderstanding would never have happened. It was quite as much his fault as it was anyone else's!

"I shouldn't have thought that hearing Mass on a transistor counted for much in the salvation stakes," she said disagreeably.

"Because you haven't thought about it at all," he answered pleasantly."

Her mouth trembled and she looked away from him to conceal it. "I'm sorry," she said. "Greeks are very devout, aren't they?"

"Perhaps. It was the Church that conserved all we held dear during the four hundred years or so we spent as a Turkish province. The richness of the liturgy holds the whole meaning of life for us."

She blinked. "I've said I'm sorry," she repeated.

Then, deciding that confession would be good for her soul, she added, "It was a bait, if you must know—not very well-chosen bait, I admit, but I wanted to make you rise!" Her penitence turned to impatience. "You deserved something—following me to Symi! Am I never to be left alone again?"

"Not if that's what you want? I thought you were looking rather lonely when I came up to you just now."

And she had been! She had been quite unbearably lonely and she couldn't imagine why. She had spent plenty of time on her own before and she had never been lonely then, so why now? She was uncomfortably aware it was all part of some great change that was taking place inside her—a change she couldn't like and which frightened her half to death. It consisted of yearning for something she wouldn't put a name to and couldn't understand.

"I had a lot to think about," she said aloud.

The corners of his mouth twitched irrepressibly. "Your grandmother?"

And him too! "She forgets that I'm English and—"

"And female? And therefore inconsistent?"

"No, not that!" she denied fiercely. "But being English, I can't accept anyone else's right to take over my life and—and put me in such an impossible situation! How could you?" she added, her reproach made all the more frantic by the tears that rushed unbidden into her eyes, making it impossible to see his face.

"There are compensations in most things," he said gently. "I think *agapí*, you are hungry again! You always look on the black side of life when you are hungry. It's a good thing I am on hand to feed you!"

"I am *not* hungry!"

"Mrs. Barron said you ate no breakfast at all so of course you are hungry, Eleanor *mou*. You will feel much more yourself when you have some good food inside you and a glass of wine to warm your heart!"

"Oh, Ioannis! It isn't as simple as that! The situation won't go away if I bury my head in the sand, will it?" She saw that he hadn't understood the allusion and muttered something about ostriches, thus adding to his confusion. "Oh, Ioannis, how can you want to *marry* me?"

It was out now, lying between them like an unexploded bomb. But Eleanor couldn't regret her moment of courage. She had to know why! *She had to!*

Ioannis shrugged his shoulders, a glint in his light green-grey eyes as he studied her, noting the quick changes of expression on her face with a pleasure that brought the colour rushing up her cheeks.

"I am old to be unmarried," he said at last. "I want sons of my own to follow in my footsteps, and a woman in my house and in my bed. At the same time, Kostas wished to settle your future and told me you would not come to the marriage empty-handed. Not only is there the house—"

"That you can't possibly want! You can't live in *two* houses at the same time! Not even you can do that!"

"When our family expands we may need the extra space," he returned calmly. "In the meantime your grandmother wishes to return to Rhodes. It will be convenient for her to live in the house until we have need of it."

Eleanor took a deep breath. "I won't do it!" Her

voice quivered painfully, but she was not going to hesitate now. "I have some pride and—and I won't do it!"

He looked amused, leaning back on his iron chair and laughing at her. If he had been within reach she would have wiped the smile off his face with a good, hard slap—and he would have deserved it too! He was quite abominable, and she disliked him more than anyone she had ever met! Marry him? It was ridiculous! So why was it so difficult to tell him so?

"You can't make me marry you!" she gasped in the back of her throat.

"I don't think it will come to that." He smiled at her.

"But, Ioannis—I don't want to marry anyone!"

The look he gave her was indulgent and very explicit. It set her heart rocketing against her ribs and turned her mouth dry. It was a look that was very male and tinged with triumph. Oh, how she wished he wouldn't look at her like that! It was—it was indecent!

"It would be a pity if you didn't marry," he said. "But as it will never happen, I refuse to shed any tears about it! You were made for marriage, *agapí mou,* and I mean to see that you come into your destiny with me!"

"I won't—I *can't* listen to you!" She had no breath left in her body, only a shocking excitement that perhaps he meant what he said. "You must see that I can't?"

"Nothing of the sort!" he retorted. "I can see you are hungry, and a little confused too, perhaps. You don't really know what you do want, do you, my Eleanor? You may think your English ways are always the best ones, but we too, in Greece, have been arranging our lives very satisfactorily for generations past. Your grandmother is wholly Greek: have you thought you may be more Greek than you have allowed for with your talk of pride and independence?"

"Not Greek enough to marry you!" she burst out.

"Nor English enough to refuse to honour your family's word! They have promised you to me, Eleanor Stewart, and I shall hold you all to that. I am warning you!" He stood up and smiled at her, for all the world as though they had been discussing nothing more explosive than the weather. She forced herself to make one last try to make him listen to her.

"I can earn quite enough to meet my needs! I have been trained to earn my own living, you know!"

He put out a hand, ruffling her hair and tracing the line of her nose as if she had been a child. "I was not talking about money, girl. I was talking about your need to be a wife and mother. You can't do that alone, and you wouldn't want to if you could!"

He took her by the hand and jerked her to her feet, putting an arm right round her to lead her firmly across the quay to the shaded tables of the restaurant. His body was hard and unyielding against hers. Again, she wondered what it would be like to have him closer still, startling herself with her own thoughts. It was all his fault, she excused herself, for speaking more frankly about such things than anyone she had ever known— and he hadn't pretended once that he thought he need fall in love before he married! Anyone would do! Even *she* would do, and he didn't know her at all, let alone love her, or feel affectionate towards her. Not that she was going to marry him of course, but she couldn't help thinking that she might very well be surprised by joy if she did! And if that was serendipity, she didn't care!

He gave her a quick squeeze and released her. "What's the matter now?" he asked her.

"I don't think I could!" she said wildly.

He raised his eyebrows, laughing at her, the glint in his eyes more pronounced even than before. "Couldn't what?"

"Not without love," she said helplessly. "I'm not cold-blooded enough for that. It would be a very odd kind of marriage!"

"You think too much—and always about things you know nothing about," he taunted her.

"And you do know, I suppose?" she countered. "I suppose you know all about it?"

"I have known my fair share of your sex—"

"Then why didn't you marry one of *them?*"

An amused smile curved his lips, revealing his strong, white teeth. "Does it matter? I didn't marry any of them and now I mean to marry you, with your grandmother's blessing and a dowry from your Uncle Kostas to boot!"

"But you don't—you *can't* love me!" she protested. "How can you want a wife you don't love and maybe won't even like very much when you get to know her?"

"Love!" he exclaimed, with such scorn that she blinked. "You don't know what you're talking about. Love is something which grows between a man and woman and which in time we shall have in abundance, I promise you. What you want is romance! But when it dies what will you have left? The cold remains of a fairy story—"

"I refuse to listen to you!" She cut him off. "It's probably because you're Greek that you don't understand—"

"I understand very well!" He interrupted her in his turn. "I am a man and you are a woman, and it is good for men and women to live together, to make children between them, and to complete each other's lives. I have chosen to marry you. Let that be enough for you until we can be together and I can make you happy to be my wife. Is it agreed?"

Agreed? No, it was not agreed! She was going back to England and she would never see him again! And, besides, nothing would induce her to live in the kind of house she had inhabited these last few days, with no proper cooking facilities and none of the comfort she was accustomed to—not even a proper bed to lie on! That last made her colour up defiantly.

"Well?" he roared at her, holding her chair for her and propelling her down onto it with a hand on her shoulder. Her flesh burned beneath his fingers despite the cotton cloth of her shirt. She sat down with as much dignity as she could muster, refusing to meet his eyes lest that knowing look should still be there, mocking her efforts to escape from a fate they both knew it was not within her to resist.

Ioannis reached his hand across the table and took possession of hers to make sure he had her whole attention.

Eleanor was forced to look at him then. The

grey-green eyes were kind, but very, very firm. She would have to answer him with something and she hadn't the faintest idea what to say.

"I don't know," she said foolishly.

"But you are going to marry me?"

She threaded her fingers through his, marvelling at how much she liked the feel of his skin against hers. She had never much liked to touch anyone before. She raised her eyes to his, seeking his help, but he only waited, endlessly patient, determined to make her say the words for herself.

"I can't think what my father will say!" she said.

Chapter Five

Her grandmother was sitting on the rocking chair in the courtyard, exactly as Eleanor had left her.

"How did your day go?" Mrs. Barron asked her with gentle irony.

Eleanor looked deliberately vague. "It went," she murmured.

"That tells me a lot! I suppose Ioannis did catch up with you?"

Eleanor turned on her grandmother with real anger. "Did you tell him where I was going? Because, if you did, it was bad of you—"

"How could I, my dear? I don't recollect you telling me where you were going, though Ioannis seemed to think he knew exactly where you'd go. Odd that, don't you think? He must know you very well to be able to read your mind like that!"

Eleanor felt crosser than ever. "He doesn't! He can't!" she said, more to herself than to the older woman. *"How could he?"*

"Mmm." Her grandmother squinted up at her, shading her eyes from the evening sun. "That young man has a great deal to recommend him if you ask me. I almost envy you—"

"Envy me? For what? Because you and Uncle Kostas have put me in an impossible situation? If you wanted to come back to Rhodes so badly why did you have to involve me? I've spent the whole day trying to explain things as they really are—and *it's all your fault!* You got me into this, you'll have to get me out again!"

"Are you sure you want to be got out?" Mrs. Barron enquired. "When you came in just now, I could have sworn there was a glow to you I don't remember seeing before!"

Eleanor glared at her. "But, Grandma—" she began in a suffocated voice. "You don't understand! He—he's quite impossible!"

Her grandmother was completely unmoved. "In what way?" she asked comfortably. "I don't think I would describe him as impossible—even from your point of view he has a great deal to recommend him and I suspect you know it! Be as indignant as you like with him, Eleanor, but don't expect to impress me with such protestations. You like him very well, and we both know it, so don't pretend to me you don't!"

"Grandma!"

Her grandmother struggled to her feet, her face full of a grim humour that made Eleanor blink. "What now?"

"Liking is a long way from loving, and it's usual to be in love with the man one is going to marry! I won't—"

"Tell that to him, my dear. Don't waste your breath on me! It is he you have to convince. Tell him—if he'll listen to you!" She laughed harshly, enjoying her young relative's consternation. "He'll be a fool if he does, and he's no fool, my dear, so you may as well make the best of things." She laughed again. "As you will, I'm sure of that! To have such a husband can't be all bad, can it?"

Eleanor refused to answer. She had already found out for herself that Ioannis was unlikely to listen to the words she spoke to him. He had a way of looking at her that had seriously undermined her concentration whenever she had been on the point of making it clear that as a modern, young Englishwoman she expected to be treated as a person with rights and principles, not as a commodity to be disposed of in any way which suited him best.

He hadn't listened at all! She hadn't actually promised to marry him—not yet!—and she wasn't going to in the future either, but he had shown no signs of considering that a necessary preliminary to making her his wife. As far as he was concerned her fate was signed and sealed and she would be delivered to him as a matter of course as soon as he could arrange for the marriage ceremony to take place.

"I don't know what my father will say!" she had cried out, and she was ashamed to remember she had been holding his hand at the time, as much to give her courage as because he had seemed to expect it.

"He'll be glad to be rid of you," he had retorted, suppressing a laugh at her expense. "Most men like to see their daughters successfully married!"

"Successfully! To a foreigner that no one has ever heard of before?" The back of her neck had prickled with sudden embarrassment. In Greece it was she who was the foreigner and he who was at home. "He would prefer me to marry an Englishman," she had added primly, pursing up her lips to add emphasis to what she knew would be her father's attitude. "I'm sorry, but he would!"

"And his daughter? What does she prefer?"

There had been a wealth of affectionate amusement in his voice that had defeated her before she had really got into her stride. *What did she prefer?* What would anyone prefer? Certainly not to be neatly packaged, tied up with string, and handed over to a man she didn't know, in exchange for a home for her grandmother. She had far too much good, honest, *English* pride to accept such a fate willingly.

"I—" she had said, and then she had begun again, "You can't want to marry me either! The whole thing is too ridiculous for words! I'll tell my grandmother so!"

He had looked her then in that certain way, his eyes glinting with the reflection of his own thoughts—none of them had boded her any good!—and his certainty that she didn't mean a word of what she had been saying.

"Marriages have been arranged this way since the beginning of time," he had said at last. "Why should it be any worse for you than for any other woman?"

She hadn't been able to believe her ears. "It isn't done that way now!" she had exclaimed when she could.

He had smiled then, dismissing her objections as if they had no more importance than the chattering of a child. "It is here!" he had told her, and he had squeezed her hand that, remarkably, was still clinging to his. "You'll get used to our ways in time and be happy!" The glint in his eyes had become very marked and she had felt herself blushing like a fool. "You're a woman first, *agapi*, and only English after that!" He had paused with a deliberation that had made her catch her breath, bringing a cruel curve to his lips. "And not wholly English at that!" he had added, a thread of amusement running through his words. And then he had dismissed the whole conversation as if it had held no further interest for him, releasing her hand at the same moment and studying the menu with a concentration she hadn't dared to try and breach.

Afterwards they had sailed back to Rhodes in his *caique* and there had been no opportunity to bring up the subject again.

"Well?" her grandmother prompted her.

Eleanor came back to the present with a bump. "Wh-what did you say?" she stammered.

Mrs. Barron's sardonic expression was suddenly unbearable to her, but she had no opportunity to say so for the older woman made no secret of her delight in the way things were going.

"Will you want your parents and English relatives here for the wedding?" she asked.

"You can't be serious!" Eleanor reproached her.

Her English relatives? Whatever next? Was she now to have her nationality snatched away from her along with everything else? "Aren't you taking a great deal for granted?" she asked.

Her grandmother chuckled. "No more than you! What makes you think you will hold out against Ioannis? He is all man, that one, and a slip of a girl like you is no match for him! Spend your energies on learning how to be a better sailor, my dear, that's my advice! His patience won't survive your breaking up his boat for him as you nearly did this evening when you brought her in!"

That had been an awkward moment. Eleanor was prepared to admit it. She hadn't the remotest idea of what all the bits and pieces of a boat were called in English, let alone in Greek, and his shouted commands had only served to confuse her still further.

"I'll learn," she said doggedly.

"If he'll teach you!" her grandmother grunted. "There isn't room for any clumsy hands on a boat, my girl, as you'll very soon discover! You think about that for a while, Eleanor Stewart, and draw your own conclusions about sailing the seas of matrimony with a man like Ioannis Nikkolides!"

"I'm trying," she said aloud, "not to think of matrimony at all! I'm not going to marry at all!"

Her grandmother smiled a secret smile and turned her back on her. "That'll be the day!" she mocked. "How good are you with your needle, girl? I'm embroidering a motif on the linen that will form part of your dowry. Would you care to give me a hand?"

Mrs. Barron could embroider like an artist. Eleanor was lost in admiration when she saw the neat pattern her grandmother had invented, consisting of roses, for the name of Rhodes; deers, both stags and does, as the symbol of the island; and the initials E and I intertwined in both the Latin and Greek scripts.

"You shouldn't do this for me!" Eleanor burst out, gulping down the lump that insisted on rising in her throat. She could see for herself the very real love and affection with which her grandmother was carrying out the task. "Grandma, I can't marry him!"

Mrs. Barron picked up her needle and threaded it with the thick cotton she had risen to fetch from her room. She patted her granddaughter awkwardly on the shoulder, her own eyes bright with unshed tears.

"I'd do a great deal more than this for you, Eleanor. Take my advice, and cry it all out of your system—all the doubts and fears you keep dreaming up to frighten yourself with—and then put it all behind you and start to enjoy being courted like any other young girl! He means to have you—and I don't blame him. A kind heart is better than great beauty in a wife any day!"

Eleanor winced. "Did *he* say I wasn't beautiful?" she demanded.

Her grandmother knotted her thread without looking at her. "Why should you mind if he did?"

"I don't!" Eleanor denied. But she did. She minded very much indeed. "It isn't fashionable to have curly hair," she added with a spurt of temper, "but we can't all have long, blonde hair, falling to our waists—"

"Or eyes like chips of blue ice," her grandmother put in calmly.

"Mine are dark!" Eleanor rounded on her. "And Sonia's are too!"

"Were we talking about Sonia?" her grandmother retorted unanswerably. "If you're not going to help with this, my dear, I suggest you take yourself off and have a swim before supper. It will cool you down after the heat of the day."

Eleanor felt as little like swimming as she did in taking up her needle and copying the device Mrs. Barron had traced onto the corners of half a dozen sheets on the table. Who had time for such nonsense in these days of noniron materials and convenience clothing? Yet somehow the gesture was unbearably sweet to her, although it tied the knots tighter that bound the strings her grandmother was pulling to make her granddaughter fall in with her plans.

The sea was as warm as the evening air. Eleanor stood waist-deep in the water and watched the sky redden, turn a pearly pink, and then darken to the uniform purple of night. She could see Ioannis on his *caique*, unravelling the chaos she had made of the sails and the ropes she believed were more correctly referred to as "sheets." His torso, naked and bronzed, gleamed in the last of the evening light as his muscles rippled and took the strain of the heavy weights of canvas he was furling about the mast and boom. She remembered the feel of those same hands against hers and she turned away, trembling in every limb.

She struck out for a distant finger of land that formed

one of the limits of the small bay. It was good to feel the caress of the water against her flesh as she put more effort into her strokes, determined to think no more of Ioannis for the time being. It lent her a spurious strength that faltered and drained away as she glanced over her shoulder and saw Ioannis had gone from the deck of the *caique*. She bit her lip. She would not think of him again!

"You shouldn't be swimming alone after dark," his voice came over the water to her.

"It isn't dark yet!" What had it got to do with him when she went swimming? "Mind your own business!" she added at a shout, kicking out at his approaching wake with something approaching panic lest he should catch up with her.

A couple of long, languid strokes and he was beside her.

"You are my business, *karthia mou*," he said in her ear. "Be still and see if you can touch the ground with your feet. If you go on splashing around like that, you're more likely to drown than reach the land alive!"

"Why should you care?" she gasped out.

"I'll tell you in my own time, Eleanor. Suppose you tell me what you're in such a fright about? Are you afraid I'm going to seduce you before I marry you?"

"Don't be silly!" she said, trying desperately to stand upright. Then she lost her footing, and swallowed a great deal of salt water because she had left her mouth open.

He put a hand beneath her elbow and guided her to the shore, eyeing her with a mocking smile. "You had better come in to shore with me without any more ridiculous struggling," he commented.

"Why should I?" she countered, floundering along beside him. "Suppose I like swimming out here?"

"Because I say so," he replied irritatingly. "And because I want a wife who does what she is told!"

"I am not your wife! I live my own life! And I see no reason to change it!"

His grip tightened on her shoulders and she wriggled away from him, trying to release herself from his bruising fingers.

"You won't be living your own life from now on!" he ground out. He hadn't spoken at all loudly, but his words found their mark and reverberated round her brain as if he had shouted them. "You'll be living mine!"

"I won't!" she declared with passion. "I won't do it!"

He lifted his head, his mouth curling at the corners with a faint smile. He was very, very sure of himself.

"You have no choice. I mean to marry you, and marry you I will, Eleanor *mou*, so put your claws away and make up your mind to accept the inevitable. You won't find it so terrible. Do you think your grandmother would have agreed to something that was not to your benefit? She is very fond of you and naturally wants your happiness. Would she have done anything to jeopardise that, do you think? She and your uncle accepted me as your husband on your behalf—"

"They had no right to do so!"

"You think not? Nevertheless, the arrangement stands and you had better make the best of it." He gave her a little shake, his smile broadening into one of a very masculine triumph. "Your reluctance makes a very pretty spectacle, *agapí*, but it is also a challenge—

a challenge I may enjoy! What man does not enjoy making a pretty woman his own? Do you think it will be different with you?"

Her eyes widened, darkening with some unnamed emotion. "But you don't think I am pretty," she objected. "You told Grandma as much!"

"You are well enough," he responded.

"Thanks very much! If you think so little of me I wonder you should want—want to—"

"Make love to you?" He laughed harshly. "I have wanted that from the first moment I saw you!"

She was shaken to the core. "But you hadn't seen me when you agreed to marry me," she pointed out. It was becoming increasingly hard to make sense of anything he said, let alone understand herself! Her emotions blew hot and cold and she had as much control over them as she had over him—and that was none at all! "Ioannis, please let me go!"

"I would, if I were physically repellent to you, but I'm not, am I?"

She fought to answer him, striving earnestly to find the words that would convince him that he meant nothing to her at all. But she could not do it. She would never love him, she thought, she couldn't do that, if only because he was Greek and foreign and quite different from any other man she had ever known. But neither did he fail to attract her. It was an ephemeral, perhaps even a wanton, attraction, but it was there nevertheless, and she could not deny it. She was curious to know what it would be like to be held close against him, to have him kiss her, even to have him make love to her. There was a little bit of her that would welcome it, and that was so shocking to her that she felt quite weak at the knees and hoped she was not going to emulate some tiresome Victorian heroine and faint away at his feet.

"I thought not," he said, and there was a decided threat in his voice.

She opened her mouth to defy him further, but no sound came. She couldn't think of anything more to say, nothing that he wouldn't remember and fling in her face at the first opportunity.

She heard him laugh again and she gulped, her heart in her mouth, willing herself to find the strength to run away from him while she still could. But she was too late to do anything of the kind. He swept her into his arms, not caring how or where he held her, and he kissed her with a ruthless efficiency that sent every thought out of her head except the need to make it easier for him to explore her soft lips and to mould her shape more closely to his own.

When he let her go, he had wiped his face clear of all expression, even the basic one of triumph. He might have been a stranger to her, so remote had he become.

"Go home to your grandmother," he told her. "You'll catch a cold if you stay out here without a wrap. Go home, *agapí,* and stay out of trouble!"

Chapter Six

The marriage drew inexorably nearer. As far as Eleanor was concerned it was the calm before the approaching storm—a storm she could only survive with dignity if she pretended to herself that it was not happening to her at all, but to someone quite other, someone who had never expected anything better from her marriage than a passive acceptance of a partner in life arranged for her by someone else and whom, more often than not, she actively disliked. Or did she? There lay the rub. She wasn't at all sure she did dislike him; indeed, she was almost sure she did nothing of the kind.

Nor did Ioannis do anything to make things easier for her. He had a way of standing, leaning against the entrance of the courtyard, and watching her. He seldom said anything to her, just watched everything she did, his face a blank or occasionally mocking when she made a mess of her grandmother's instructions as to how she should cook the food on the primitive fire, or carry out any of the other tasks that were considered part and parcel of any Greek girl's life, especially one who was shortly to become a bride.

"Haven't you anything else to do?" she had asked him once, exasperated. "What do you do anyway?"

"Do?"

"Yes, do! I suppose you do work occasionally?" she had said with unwonted sarcasm. "You can't do nothing all the time!"

"I work, yes," he had answered, his eyebrows rising in open amusement. "I plan to keep you in the comfort you are accustomed to. You don't have to worry yourself about that!"

She had been annoyed that he had thought it was that that had goaded her into asking the question. She had shrugged her shoulders. "I've never seen you do any work," she had claimed.

"You will," he had answered quietly.

"And meanwhile I have to do everything? Some comfort! Why don't you modernise these houses—if we have to live in a folk museum? You could at least light the fires in the mornings! I can't ask my grandmother to do it forever!"

"No, you can't!" he had agreed promptly. "You're a slow learner when it comes to the domestic arts,

84

Eleanor Stewart. You'll have to apply yourself better, won't you? You still have a great deal to learn and not many more days in which to practise!"

Her grandmother had invited Ioannis to share their evening meal. He had accepted with sardonic amusement.

"You can get the meal!" she had declared to her grandmother. "I'll have nothing to do with it!"

Mrs. Barron had merely smiled, ignoring the mutinous set of her granddaughter's mouth.

Of course it had been Eleanor who had cooked the meal in the end. She had done it alone too, her grandmother choosing to go out at the last moment to visit a friend of her girlhood in the neighbouring village.

"For heaven's sake, Eleanor," she had said on her departure, "don't go to pieces now, girl! You can make a salad just as well as anyone else, and the only other thing there is to do is to roast the meat and cook the rice—"

"It's the fire!" Eleanor had protested in agony. "I never know how hot it's going to be! One day the meat is raw and another a burnt offering!"

"More often the latter," Mrs. Barron had grunted. "If you can't manage, Eleanor, ask Ioannis to help you! You can't stay tied to my apron strings forever!"

Fortunately for Eleanor's peace of mind, the fire had responded to her ministrations better than she had dared hope. She had even remembered to cool the wine and to set a dish of yogurt to thicken well in time for it to form that thick, white skin that made the homemade variety so much more delicious than most shop-bought equivalents. The last thing she would have done would have been to ask Ioannis' help! She would starve first before she ever asked his help again!

And now here he was, seated across the table from her in the moonlight, the flickering candle between them, now lighting, now shading the firm features of his face and hiding the quality of his contempt for her as he helped himself to the lamb kebab she had put before him.

"Three more days," he said suddenly, addressing her directly for the first time since he had walked into their ill-lit courtyard, his trousers clean and beautifully pressed, and his cheesecloth shirt accentuating the breadth of his shoulders and the strength of his body.

"So?" she responded, congratulating herself on the coolness of that icy syllable.

"Kyria Athena tells me you are suffering from nerves—that you are becoming quite impossible to live with."

It was a second or two before Eleanor recognised her grandmother as being the Kyria Athena. Was that really her name? Funny, but she had never thought of her as having a Christian name before. Mrs. Barron, yes; Grandma, all the time; but had anyone ever called her Athena? Her grandfather certainly hadn't! It had been—

"Her name is Hatti," she said aloud. "I've never heard her called Athena before!"

"No?" It seemed he could be every bit as icily polite as she. "In England she may have been called Hatti, here in Rhodes her name has always been Athena and always will be. She is proud to have been called after the personification of wisdom—a quality her granddaughter would do well to cultivate, don't you think?"

"Perhaps." One could hardly deny that, she thought wretchedly, but she didn't like having it pointed out to her all the same. She wished her grandmother were here now. She had promised to be home in ample time to help entertain Ioannis and yet there was still no sign of her.

"She isn't coming," Ioannis said, picking up her thoughts as easily as if she had spoken them aloud. "I asked her to stay away for the evening. She'll be back in time to chaperon you for the night but, until then, we have only each other to consider." His eyes met hers and refused to allow her to look away. "Isn't that nice?" he added mendaciously. "We can behave like any other engaged couple in England, without any protective eye being kept on your honour. Your grandmother was very cooperative. Living in England all these years, some of your permissive ways must have brushed off on her after all. She was quite willing to leave you in my care for a few hours although there are three more days to go before we become man and wife."

She started up onto her feet. "I won't stay here with you alone!" She resented the amusement he hadn't bothered to hide from her, and resented even more the futility of her own retort. How could she help but stay where she was? Nor was it going to do her any good to sound as frightened as she felt of his intentions towards her.

Tears jerked into her eyes and she turned her face away lest he should see them. "I don't see why you should want me here at all!" she said, her voice made husky with the emotion of the moment. "Why do you?"

He raised his glass to her in a mocking salute. "Not for your cooking, *karthia mou,* improved though it has under Kyria Athena's tuition. You have been spoilt with your western gadgets and labour-saving devices, but the pleasures of the table rate a poor second to the pleasures of the bed, wouldn't you say? And there your tuition lies with me. You will find me an able master—"

"A practised one no doubt!" she retorted.

"And you care about that?"

She could not meet the twin reflections of candlelight in his eyes. If he had wanted to embarrass her, he had certainly succeeded! And she was the modern young lady from the permissive lands of the West, whereas he—what he was didn't bear thinking about!

"No," she said, "I don't care at all!"

He said nothing to that, but his eyes travelled over her, exploring all the details of her shape in silence. Defensively, she moved away from the light of the candle, scowling down at the food on the table. She had done her best to make it appetising, cooking those dishes which she had come to know from her grandmother were his favourites, and she might just as well not have bothered. Indeed, she couldn't understand why she had! She had no particular ambition to please him!

"I haven't seen that dress before," he said at last.

"No." She couldn't have said another word to save

her life. She stared down at her hands, her back very straight, and licked her lips with a nervousness that was oddly appealing if she had but known it.

"You should wear it more often," he suggested.

She raised her head. "Perhaps I will. I only finished making it this afternoon. There are such pretty dresses to be had in Greece and—and I thought I'd make myself one. It's much cheaper than buying, you see."

"I like it. Did you do the embroidery too?"

Her fingers went automatically to the extravagant pattern on the front, a modified replica of the one her grandmother had designed for her bridal linen.

"Yes."

"Very nice!" he approved. "It has a strong flavour of Rhodes about it. If you chose it, you must be happier here than you want me to believe." He leaned forward, tracing the design on the top of her bodice with a long, lean forefinger. "An E—and do I detect an I? An I for Ioannis?"

"It's—it's part of the general design! It isn't meant to be an I, or anything in particular!" She pulled away from him, rocking her chair dangerously in her panic, and gasped in fright as she thought she might be going to fall. His fingers met hers, steadied her, and took her hand in his, drawing her up to her feet and into the circle of his arms.

"Why not an I for Ioannis? It would be a fitting recognition on your part of your husband-to-be!" The cajolery in his voice made her blink. Why should he want such an acknowledgement? Why should it matter to him what she should choose to embroider on her clothes or anywhere else?

"Won't you even give me that much?" he said against her lips.

"No!"

"Are you quite, quite certain of that?" His lips took hers with a gentleness that undermined her resistance as no amount of force could have done. "Eleanor?"

Her mouth trembled into a denial, but the words would not come out. The sweet toll of his lips drowned her defiance in a new, previously untried excitement that caught her unawares and had her straining against him, seeking more of the same. He held her closer, and closer still, his hands at first soothing and then a part of the demand he was making for her complete surrender to his caresses.

When he let her go, she gazed up at him with a lost wonder in her eyes. "Ioannis—" she breathed.

His smile was as cruel as his lips had been warm and kind against hers. "You're no different from any other woman, Eleanor mine, and you won't hold out against me for long! Three more days! That's all you have to rebuild your defences against me, my reluctant bride of the sun! *Three more days*—if I can wait so long!"

Three more days. Bride of the sun. His words spun round her head and she could make no sense of them. *Bride of the sun?* A burning blush crept up her throat and cheeks to her hair line and she stood absolutely motionless, scarcely feeling the warm pressure of his hands against her back.

"A lot can happen in three whole days," she said.

Nothing did. Her family, apprised of her wedding plans, were at first shocked by her haste and then effusive in their apologies for not making the trip to Rhodes to see her married. Eleanor was not much surprised by their lack of interest. For a time she had played with the idea that they might rescue her from the predicament in which she found herself, but a more realistic assessment of her family's capacity for interest in anyone else's affairs but their own convinced her they would genuinely wish her well, regret she had decided to live so far away from them, and then forget all about her except for brief intervals when her mother would mean to put pen to paper but would seldom do so and her father would declaim with sorrow that his elder daughter had elected to marry a foreigner whom he had never even met.

It wasn't that they were any more self-centred than anybody else, Eleanor told herself, it was simply that they were so deeply absorbed in their own interests that they had no energy left for worrying about the doings of anyone else. They had been like that with her grandmother: delighted to see her whenever she appeared on their doorstep, but out of sight had very soon been out of mind.

The day before the wedding, she felt the need to escape the claustrophobic atmosphere of the two neighbouring houses more than ever. Mrs. Barron had intended she should spend the day resting, washing her hair, and being pampered as if she were the fat goose to be slaughtered for the feast on the following day. That was how she felt too! Her whole being quivered whenever she allowed herself to dwell, even for a moment, on what the ceremony was going to mean in her life.

Somehow or other, before that dreadful hour came upon her, she had to reconcile herself with that future and, to do that, she felt a yearning need to be alone, to be free of her grandmother's suggestive self-satisfaction in her granddaughter's fate, and, most of all to be free of Ioannis' eyes on her and to kick up her heels and enjoy herself like any other young girl on holiday in Rhodes.

Dressed in an ancient pair of jeans and a shirt that had faded from a bright blue to an insignificant grey with much washing, she slipped out of the house and started walking as fast as she could down the road. It was marvellous to be out in the air, in the hot sunshine and to be answerable to no one for the long hours of the afternoon that stretched ahead of her and that she would spin out like a child on a spree, released unexpectedly from school, with delight and keen anticipation for anything that might happen to her.

There was no sign of Ioannis, which brought a sigh of relief to her lips. To her grandmother she might have explained her urge to come to terms with herself before the next day; to Ioannis she knew she could not.

Most of the traffic on the road was tourists mounted on motor scooters, the man in front and the girl behind, clinging onto the driver for dear life. They were fair and laughed a great deal, wrapped up in a confident happiness she couldn't share. It made her feel lonelier than ever.

The windmills, however, would have delighted her at any time. Not the newer ones that reminded her of pictures she had seen of the Australian outback, but the typically Greek ones, built of stone, with canvas sails that were as often as not furled tightly against the wooden struts they turned when they were working. Now and again she would catch sight of one moving ponderously in the onshore breeze and she would stop and stare at it for a while, eager to etch its movement into her mind's eye.

One such windmill attracted her attention at the same moment as one of the tourist scooters drew up beside her. She shielded her eyes from the sun with her hand and pretended not to have noticed the young man who had come to a stop only a yard or so from her feet. He seemed to be alone, and his corn-coloured hair proclaimed him to be a Scandinavian, free from the restraints of home and determined to have a good time.

"*Kalimera*," he began the conversation.

Flattered to be mistaken for a Greek, Eleanor smiled at him. She wondered if she should point out to him that it was no longer morning and that it might have been more proper to wish her "Good afternoon," but then she chided herself for being pedantic and, who was she to talk, she with her ten words of Greek and an English accent one could cut with a knife?

"Hullo there!" she answered in casual dismissal.

"You are English?" he exclaimed with pleasure. "American?"

"English," she admitted. "And you?"

He shrugged, considering the answer too obvious to bother with. "English! That is very good for me! And you are on your own too." His eyes slid over her face, assessing her possibilities as far as he was concerned. "I am going to see the butterflies," he announced, and she presumed she had passed whatever test it was he had set for her in his mind. "Will you come with me?"

"What butterflies?" she asked. She was strongly tempted to go with him anyway, knowing that such a move would throw her grandmother into hysterics, and Ioannis . . . But Ioannis was tomorrow and today she belonged to herself and would make the most of it! She clenched her fists defiantly by her sides and smiled slowly and invitingly at the young Swede on his scooter. "Not that it matters," she said. "I'd love to see your butterflies!"

He told her all about them all the same. In earnest, uncertain English, he explained that up in the hills, behind the coast, was a valley that was renowned the whole world over for its butterflies. "They are all the same kind," he went on. "I think they may be moths really for they hold their wings differently from other butterflies I have seen. When they are disturbed, they rise up in a cloud of scarlet and brown. They are very beautiful." He lowered his voice, putting his young, fair face very close to hers. "The valley is secluded too, with many trees, and lots of quiet places where one can be alone—between the tour buses. It would be pleasant, no?"

"Yes," she said.

She hesitated no longer, but mounted the scooter behind him and allowed him to pull her hands round to the front of his shirt without protest. Ioannis would be furious if he could see her now. The thought gave her pleasure, but it also made her glance over her shoulder to ensure he was nowhere in sight and would never know about her last, defiant gesture before she entered the prison of marriage to him. How strange, therefore, that that prison held a fascination for her that freedom had never had. *Butterflies!* She had enough butterflies in her stomach to last her a lifetime! And if she was like this now, what was she going to be like by this time tomorrow!

They were making their way up the road for the new airport. It meant she had to hold on tight or be thrown off altogether as they fell from one pothole into another, roaring the engine to get out again, as though the noise itself was part of the pleasure of the drive. A tatty sign, bearing a picture of a butterfly, invited them to turn off the main road and take their chances with a track that led up into the hills. The roadmakers were busy here too, with great piles of stone chips taking up most of the space and reducing the traffic to chaos.

"Why are you alone here?" her companion asked her, twisting his head round so that she could hear him.

"I'm not alone," she answered. "I have my grand-mother with me—"

He was shocked by the very idea, looking at her as though she were some kind of freak, until the change of surface forced him to look ahead again and take some interest in where they were going.

"*Grandmother?* Did she wish to holiday with you?"

"She comes from here," Eleanor told him, and then

abruptly changed the subject. She didn't want her grandmother's shadow with her this afternoon. She wanted freedom and the spice of a mild adventure, instigated and carried through entirely by herself. "What are you doing on your own?"

"My girl is unwell. I think she has her eye on somebody else and has gone to the beach with him. She says she has a headache and will stay in her room all day. I don't care." He cast her a brilliant smile. "My name is Lars. What is yours?"

She told him, a little alarmed by the traces of recent rock falls from the cliff that edged one side of the road. Then, without any warning, the track branched into two, a battery of signs announcing the cost of the project of making the road and the name of the contractors, the direction of the nearest restaurant, but absolutely nothing to tell them which way they should go for the butterflies.

"We will go up," Lars decided. "The valley is high in the hills, and that one goes downhill, almost down to sea level again."

Eleanor had no choice but to go with him. He roared up the engine, skidded on some loose sand as they took the next corner on the wrong side of the road and narrowly escaped ending up under the wheels of a bus coming in the opposite direction. A great blast of horn turned the young Swede's ears pink, but his spirits rose again dramatically as they shot round another corner and found themselves face to face with the entrance to the Butterfly Valley.

A man was selling figs close by where they parked the

scooter. Not many of them were ripe, but Lars lingered by the stall anyway, trying to make up his mind whether it would be a nice gesture to buy some for his girlfriend. "Perhaps she really has a headache," he tried to convince himself, "though I think not. No one man can ever satisfy her!"

Lucky her! Eleanor thought. *She* had never met Ioannis if she could think that! She would like to see Ioannis Hyperion Nikkolides sharing a woman with anyone else!

"Lars, I didn't bring any money with me. I didn't think I'd need any. Do you mind paying for me as well?"

He put his hand reluctantly into his pocket. "You should never go out without money," he lectured her, handing her the modest coin she would need to buy her ticket. She thanked him and his face brightened, and he laughed with a faint shrug of his shoulders. "It is beautiful, isn't it?" he asked. "We shall have a good time, no?"

Eleanor nodded her agreement, her mouth curving into a smile that froze on her lips. Leaning over the counter, talking to the man on the other side was a figure she could not mistake, not if she were not to see him again for a hundred years.

"Ioannis!" she breathed.

He stood up straight, negligently, as if he had all the time in the world, and came towards her—and Lars. His Swedish was evidently as good as his English, and he was kind to the young Swede as he plainly was not going to be with her. As white as a sheet, she watched

97

him exchange a brief, masculine handshake with Lars, and then he turned to her.

"You won't need the young man's drachmas," he said in a voice that effectively removed the last of her smile. "I have your ticket here, Eleanor *mou*, with mine!"

Chapter Seven

The silence was unbearable. There wasn't a murmur to be heard anywhere in the valley. Where Lars had got to, Eleanor couldn't imagine. She and Ioannis might have been the only two people left on earth—and he looked as though he was enjoying it as little as she was.

Some steps led up to a catwalk made from a lot of bark-covered branches nailed across wooden supports. The sunlight falling through the struts made patterns on the water below. It was pretty, but the silence was intolerable to her. Apart from the sound of a waterfall, there was only silence. Not a bird sang; not a person spoke.

Eleanor glanced nervously at Ioannis. His face in profile looked stern and unyielding and she felt unaccountably guilty. After all, what did it matter if she had hitched a lift with the young Swede? It was the sort of thing other people did every day. Why, a few days ago, in England, if the occasion had arisen, she would have done it without a thought as to the consequences.

"How did you know I was here?"

The sound of her voice, deep and husky, startled three or four butterflies into leaping into life, flashes of scarlet against the dark green of the trees.

Ioannis looked at her for a long moment in silence, assessing the mixture of defiance and guilt that was written on her freshly tanned face. She writhed under his gaze, wishing she had not spoken after all. Perhaps the silence would have proved a better defence against him in the end. Perhaps she should have waited for him to speak first. She turned her face away from him, caught up in the dilemma of her own lack of resolution. Now that she had spoken, shouldn't she say something more, something that would convince him that she didn't care what he thought of her?

But she did! She cared with every fibre of her being and, if she were not very careful, she knew she would rush into a long speech of self-justification as to just why she had accepted a lift to the valley from Lars. He had made no demands on her, not like Ioannis did just by standing there and looking at her. Lars had meant a means of transport, nothing more than that.

"I didn't know," Ioannis answered at last. "I was here myself and I saw your arrival." His mouth tightened. "That young man might have killed you, going under the wheels of that bus like that!"

"You were here? But what were you doing here?"

"I wanted to get out of the house," he said. "I hate waiting, and with your grandmother running in and out all the time, and I don't know how many other women helping her to make all the arrangements for tomorrow, I couldn't stand it any longer. I came away to get a breath of fresh air!"

"So did I!" Eleanor confided with a rush. "I hate waiting around too and, even more, I hate being told to rest! It makes me nervous!"

He looked amused. "What have you to be nervous about? Don't you think I'll look after you properly?"

She looked down into the shadowed waters seeing nothing. "I don't know anything about you," she complained. "I've been trying not to think about it, but I can't put it off forever—only, tomorrow doesn't seem quite real, does it?"

"It seems real enough to me," he answered her. "Perhaps I've had longer than you have to get used to the idea."

"I never shall!" she said with a violence that made the whole catwalk shake.

He put a hand over hers, pressing her fingers down hard against the bark of the balustrade. "Have you any choice, *agapí*? After tomorrow it will be your life and you will get used to it just by living it. That happens to most women after marriage after all."

Tears filled her eyes and trickled out of the corners. She wiped them indignantly away, annoyed by her own weakness.

"Not to people like me!" she declared. "We *choose*—" She broke off, looking at him covertly, expecting to receive his sympathy, but it seemed he had none for her. His expression was distant and hard, and her spirits sank. For a moment she had thought he understood, but he didn't! More, he didn't even care!

"You, too, have chosen, Eleanor," he said abruptly, withering the last of her hopes that he had any gentleness in his makeup. "You have chosen to answer the call of your Greek blood—it is no good looking back now over your shoulder at what might have been, *pedhi*. It's too late for that! In Greece marriage is a very serious business, the very centre of our lives, and we have a gift for making the most of life, involving our whole selves in our everyday joys and sorrows. I shall expect no less of you! Sooner or later you must find your enduring happiness in marriage to me. Let's hope it will be sooner—for your sake!"

"You're not very kind," she said, badly shaken. "Why should I be happy, married to a stranger, living in a foreign country, and—and in one of the most uncomfortable houses I've ever come across? There doesn't seem to be much in that for me!"

He lifted his hand, holding her by the chin and forcibly turning her face towards him. "Very little, if you are still determined to give nothing!" He put his forefinger across her lips in a gesture the intimacy of which set her heart racing. With an effort, she tore her eyes away from his and tried to control her breathing in case he should—in case he should *what?* See the invitation that lurked beneath the surface of doubt and uncertainty she had presented him with?

"Ioannis, I'm not Greek. I'm not at all Greek!" It was difficult to speak against his finger, more difficult still not to allow it to conjure up memories of other things he had done to her lips, the warmth and hardness of his mouth against hers, demanding a like enthusiasm from hers, and receiving it too. That was the humiliating part about it. If she went on like this, he would think she *enjoyed* his kisses.

"But you are all woman, *agapí mou!* Giving is your nature, fight against it how you may!" He patted her cheek with his free hand, his fingers trailing along the line of her jaw and coming to rest on the nape of her neck. "Your mouth was made to be kissed, and who better to have the privilege but the man you're about to marry?"

She had no choice. He was gentler than he had ever been before, kissing her eyes and both her cheeks and then, finally, her mouth. She thought her heart had stopped and that she had died in a blaze of glory. It wasn't dying as she had ever thought of it before, a slipping away into darkness and sleep, it was a new birth, bright with the dancing light of the sun, and pulsating with a new life that had little in common with what she had been before.

She was trembling when he let her go. She put her hands down on the bannister in front of her, secretly afraid her knees were going to refuse to support her any further. Here and there, a butterfly rose into the air and one of them came to rest on her shoulder, folding its orange-scarlet wings into a marbled black and brown against the cloth of her shirt.

"They can't be butterflies," she said weakly. "Butterflies put their wings together, they don't fold them away like that."

"They are called butterflies in Greek," he told her. There was a note in his voice that told her he was amused by her choice of subject, but what did he expect? That she should admit he could stir her to the depths whenever he chose? But she wouldn't! She wouldn't give an inch if she could help it! The colour came and went in her cheeks and she held onto the bar in front of her so tightly that her knuckles shone white through her skin.

Ioannis bent his head close to hers. "Are you still nervous?" he asked in her ear.

She opened her mouth to speak, but she could not. She could think of nothing except the closeness of his body to hers and the feel and the smell of him. On his looks she didn't dare dwell even for a second. If she did, those grey-green eyes of his would read her mind and he would know that he had only to put out a hand to her to make sure of his victory.

She had to say something! In a panic, she uttered a strangled sound, and the old saw came into her head to mock her, that she was hesitating again and that he who hesitates is lost. But she was already lost beyond repair. She was lost to England, family and friends; she was lost to her girlhood too, or she would be on the following day; and she was alone, except for a husband who didn't bother to pretend he was in love with her, and a grandmother who expected her to find joy in a situation which anyone could see could only lead to a kind of unhappiness she doubted she could bear. She had always had nothing but contempt for girls who fell for a physical attraction, without a thought for the more lasting aspects of love, and yet here she was, doing exactly the same, overwhelmed by a few kisses and the touch of a man's hands against her flesh.

"Ioannis, I'm sorry—"

How easy it would be to pretend to be in love with him! The thought made her blush until she felt hot all over. She looked away from him again, desperately trying to restore herself to a cool calm that would pass for a more sophisticated indifference—provided he didn't touch her again!

"Sorry?" His mockery dangerously undermined her efforts and she bit her lip. "Never be sorry, Eleanor *mou*. Don't waste your reserves on apologies! It's a weakness you can't afford—not with the enemy at your very gates!"

"I can't believe the enemy is so ruthless as to take advantage of me," she began in a voice that quivered badly.

"I have no thoughts of offering you any mercy, my dear." He cut her off, pulling on a tightly curled lock of hair with gentle fingers. "I shall enjoy the conquest of my wife, whether she comes to me willingly or not, and tomorrow I shall have the right to do so!"

"There's no need to gloat about it!" she retorted, ruffled. "It—it isn't at all gallant—"

His laughter rang through the valley, disturbing a hundred, a thousand butterflies that rose simultaneously in a shimmering cloud of bright red, in a sight so beautiful that Eleanor couldn't help wishing to see them dance before her eyes again. Somehow, by the time they were still again, much of the sting had gone out of the threat Ioannis had held out to her. That was tomorrow. Today, she had the delight of the butterflies, and she would drive everything else out of her mind, and enjoy them as best she could.

"They're beautiful!" she exclaimed, her voice softened with pleasure. "I've never seen anything like it! I wish we could make them fly up again like that! Don't you think they're beautiful?"

"Beautiful," he echoed, but he was not looking at the butterflies. He was looking at her! "We are only at the beginning of the valley here though. We can climb up to the end and, if a bus happens to come along while we're there, one of the guides will come up with them and will blow his whistle. It's like being in the centre of an autumn storm when that happens."

"I'd love to see it!" She glanced at him, hesitating, remembering too late that he had come here to escape the events of the morrow every bit as much as she had. "I expect you've seen it before though. If you don't want—I mean, I can easily go on my own. You don't have to come with me!"

"And allow you to thumb a lift back with that lunatic young man?"

"Lars?" She shrugged. "Would it matter? He's quite nice really, and he drives much better than you think. We didn't expect that awkward turning in the road."

"There would be other things you would not expect," he said in such superior tones she lowered her lashes and peeped at him through them, wondering if she dared laugh out loud. "And if you do that to anyone else but me, you'll be sorry!" he finished on an even more arrogant note. "I won't have you playing the fool, Eleanor—"

At the sound of the whistle a cloud of red and gold whirled about her head. Eleanor stepped aside to let the bus party pass and the guide, standing astride two stones in the middle of the stream below the rustic walk, smiled up at her. He raised his arms as though the sight of the butterflies rising in panic had been his own personal gift to her alone. Despite herself, Eleanor blushed as she smiled back at him and felt the warning pressure of Ioannis' fingers on her elbow.

"How many times must I tell you, Eleanor, that such looks must be kept for me!"

She was immediately indignant. "But, Ioannis, I didn't do a thing!"

His look was enough to make her lower her eyes and wonder at the painful band round her chest. He pulled her closer against him to allow the bus party to go past and then let her go, striding up the path ahead of her. As she followed him, willy nilly, she had only his back to look at: a strong, broad-shouldered back that tapered down to narrow hips and legs that moved with the ease of a natural athlete. How strange it was, she thought, that he should want to marry her! There must have been a dozen local girls who would have fallen over themselves for the chance to be Mrs. Nikkolides, so why her?

Close to the head of the valley they met the bus party going back. To look at, they could have been of any nationality, with their cotton tops patterned exactly the same as the ones she had seen for sale in England, and all with the same brands of cameras, and identical shoes. It was only when they spoke that she recognised they were French, with a natural reluctance for being hurried along by their anxious courier who had allotted a bare half-hour to the valley and was already afraid they were going to linger longer than he had allowed for.

The guide's eye fell immediately on Eleanor. With a wide grin, he swung himself down into the narrow gorge carved out by the stream and blew his whistle once again, laughing up at them. His comment was in Greek and unintelligible to her, but not to Ioannis who called back something to the man in green that was greeted by laughter and a very masculine look of appreciation as he gave Eleanor a last, lingering glance.

"What did you say to him?" she asked Ioannis, seating herself on a stone step the better to watch the butterflies settle again, blending perfectly with rocks and the bark of the trees to which they clung.

"Nothing I would care to repeat to you," he answered abruptly. "We had best go back now. Your grandmother will wonder what has become of you and there is much to be done before tomorrow."

She stared down at the butterflies, pulling a face. "Supposing I run away in the night? What will you do then?"

He squatted down beside her. "I shall find you and bring you home. Never doubt that I know how to look after my own, *yinéka mou*. Tomorrow merely sets a seal on our relationship; it was at our betrothal that you were given to me, and what I have, I keep."

She believed him. What she wanted to know was why. He had to have some reason for wanting to marry her.

"It's very strange," she said at last. "When Uncle Kostas and Grandma agreed to the marriage, I didn't even know you existed. How could I be held to that?"

"You know about me now!" He stood up, holding his hand out to her. "That excuse might have served you when you first came to Rhodes, but it won't do after the last few days. It's true we pay more attention to a girl's wishes than we used to do, but her family still has the last say in finding a suitable husband for her. Still, our marriages are mostly happy ones—as ours will be, when you have put away your doubts and allow yourself to feel instead of think. Never forget you have Greek blood in your veins as well as English!"

"Very little of it is Greek," she objected.

"Enough to make you desirable to every Greek male you meet! If anything is English, it is your mind and the way you have been taught to think. You think too much, *agapí!* Relax and enjoy what happens to you and allow yourself to be the woman you want to be!"

"I want to be free," she sighed. "Here, all I'm likely to be is the woman in your house, a part of *you* and never myself at all!"

He was amused. He hauled her to her feet and faced her down the path up which they had come, brushing down the seat of her trousers with an ungentle hand.

"Is that so bad?" he asked her. "To be possessed

completely is surely better than to be frustrated in your physical needs. If a man allows his woman to do as she pleases it can only be because he has no real interest in her—and you would not like that, I'm thinking, little Eleanor! You like to have the whole attention of a man to yourself, even if he does no more than give you pleasure by blowing his whistle to stir up the butterflies for your delight!"

She was more than a little shocked that he should speak to her like that. Such things were better never mentioned, never even thought about! She held her head up high and walked ahead of him down the path, disapproval in every line of her body. She was further disconcerted by the sound of his laughter behind her, an arrogant, conceited sound that did nothing for her comfort. She turned on him furiously, her face scarlet.

"I'm not at all as you think! What if I do like to watch the butterflies? Who wouldn't? You benefited by his blowing his whistle as much as I did—"

"But he wouldn't have done it for me!" he taunted her, still laughing.

Eleanor could have stamped her foot with rage. "How do you know?" she demanded.

He put his tongue in his cheek, a distinct gleam in his eye. "He told me so," he offered unanswerably. "He only goes to so much trouble for pretty girls who flirt with their eyes and make him feel more of a man than he did before!"

Eleanor swallowed, her anger gone. She didn't believe a word of it, of course. She wouldn't take his word for anything! "You're making it up," she accused him.

"Maybe. You'll never know, will you, my sweet? That should make you resolve to learn my language! If you don't, you'll never know what you might be missing!"

She shrugged her shoulders, turning away and continuing her way down the path. "I am a most incurious person," she claimed, crossing her fingers as though that might somehow mitigate the lie. "And I've never been much of a one for learning foreign languages. I shall probably go to my grave speaking only English, which is, after all, my native tongue!"

He said something in Greek to confuse her, and she hated him still more because she longed to know what he had said and was too proud to ask him. She turned the words over and over in her mind, finding that she knew one or two of them, having heard them several times from him before. She recognised the phrase for my woman, *yinéka mou*, and she trembled inwardly at the thought of being the woman of Ioannis. Was he right in thinking she wanted to attract his whole attention to herself? If she did, it didn't bode very well for her future happiness. She might be going to be his wife, but he didn't love her, and he had never pretended for a moment that he did. If she were to fall in love with him—

"There's another bus-load coming up," she said aloud. "I wonder what nationality they will be this time? Scandinavian? German?"

"They may be British. If they are, will you join them?"

She cast an anxious eye over the group that was climbing rapidly up the rustic path towards her. It was lowering to her self-respect, but she couldn't help hoping they would turn out to be any other nationality but British! To have to greet them, even to say no more than a polite hullo, while Ioannis stood and watched her, mocking her lack of resolution for not asking their help to escape him, was something she could very well do without.

The language they were speaking was not English, however, and she heaved a sigh of relief, hoping he hadn't noticed. The women, in unsuitable platform sandals, passed by with eyes averted; their menfolk, more open in their manners, considered both Ioannis and Eleanor, plainly curious to know what the couple was doing there. Eleanor gave them back look for look as they hurried on up the path.

"They seem to have more time to spare than the others," Eleanor commented. "And they certainly were not British!"

"No," Ioannis agreed. "A mixed collection. Probably a local tour pulling in people from a number of hotels."

Eleanor nodded. "Perhaps that's why they had no courier with them," she considered. "It's nicer being by ourselves, isn't it? I like to have time and not be hurried away from anything which catches my fancy!"

"My dear girl, I'm flattered, but not enough to encourage you into dawdling long enough to weave your spell round this guide too! You've seen all the butterflies you're going to today!"

She didn't mind his teasing this time. She even thought she caught a note of affection in his words, and that gave her such a warm feeling of contentment that she could have hugged herself with sheer happiness. She ran down the last few steps of the path, sobering almost to a halt as she reached the rustic catwalk that, despite the bark-covered struts, was slippery under the rubber soles of her shoes. As she made her way across the stream, she paused and turned back to look up at Ioannis.

"Thank you for taking me up the valley," she said shyly. "It wouldn't have been the same with Lars."

"Would it not?" he answered dryly. "He would have expected you to be properly grateful no doubt!"

She frowned. "But I am grateful! I've just said so!"

He took a step towards her, his eyes alight with an emotion that rendered her breathless. "How grateful? Grateful enough to give me the kiss Lars would have demanded from you?"

"Oh, but he wouldn't! He has a girlfriend of his own! He didn't even want to pay for my ticket. He thought I should pay for my own." She tossed her head at him, her mouth curving into a smile of naked invitation. "Swedes understand all about equality, you see!"

His arm caught her close against him. "The Greeks understand other things much better! You will find out!"

"I like being equal—"

"You'll like being my woman even more! To be unique is better than to be equal, *agapi!* Leave those who will to be the equals of men like Lars!"

Her eyelashes fanned out over her cheeks as she lowered her eyes to hide from the green-grey challenge in his. She put her hand over the one of his that was restraining her, noting how small hers looked against his. Somehow the contrast stressed the other differences between them and she looked up at him after all and saw that he had made a like comparison and was equally aware of his own strength and her feminine weakness, two halves of a single whole.

She walked with a self-conscious air to the entrance barrier, making a great play of looking at the articles and postcards they had for sale. Leaning against the counter was a young girl, her black hair coiled against her neck, a faint, very faint smile on her scarlet lips. She pulled herself upright as soon as she saw Ioannis, holding out her arms to him.

Ioannis shook his head at her, warning her of something Eleanor couldn't understand. "I'm glad you're here, Mercedes. There is someone I want you to meet!"

The black-haired girl cast him a reproachful look, and she spoke in a slow, deliberate English that was very attractive. "Ioannis, naturally you are glad to find me here as I told you I was coming!" She pouted, emphasising the softness of her well-formed lips. "I am told you have been in Rhodes for several days and yet you have not come to see me! *Philotimo* can be carried too far by someone like you! Not even I will wait forever! Your sister has been married these past three months and still you have stayed away!"

"I had other responsibilities," Ioannis explained. He held her against him and kissed her cheek and the back of her hand. "You are as lovely as ever, Mercedes! I'm surprised your father hasn't found a husband for you long before this. How have you persuaded him to make no move on your behalf?"

Mercedes' eyes flashed fire. "You know why not! I wait for you! It is well known I will have none other! First you must marry your sister before you can marry, but now you are free! You are free at last! You *must be,* Ioannis! Not even I will wait forever!"

She turned her gaze onto Eleanor, seeing her as someone attached to Ioannis for the first time. Slowly, she pointed an imperious finger at her. "Who is that? Not another sister you must marry first? That I cannot bear! *Philotimo!* It is so old-fashioned! Me, I am too modern to be concerned with such things!"

Ioannis touched her on the shoulder. "Unfortunately, I am not. Mercedes, this is Eleanor Stewart, the girl I am to marry. That is what I came to tell you. With my sister wed, I am free to marry myself, but it has been agreed that I should marry Eleanor—"

The cry that came from the Greek girl's throat drowned the remainder of his words. She sounded like a wounded animal and scarcely human at all. Horrified, Eleanor watched her, frozen to the spot by the other girl's grief. And yet not a single tear was shed and, when the cries had died away, her face was as immaculate and as beautiful as it had been before.

Down the valley came the group of tourists returning to their bus. Mercedes turned in silence and led them out into the road, counting them carefully as they mounted the steep step to get to their seats. Then, last of all, she joined them without a single, backward look. In another moment, the bus had started up and she was gone.

Chapter Eight

"What is *philotimo?*" Eleanor asked when she could say anything at all.

Ioannis recalled her presence with difficulty. He turned impatiently, his eyes flickering over her as though she were a stranger he had never seen before.

"*Philotimo?* It's a Greek concept that doesn't translate into English very well. It is a sense of honour and self-esteem that is necessary to every Rhodian man. It governs his status in his family and village, and most of all his sense of nationality. It was *philotimo* that gave us our independence and kept us as a single people under

116

both the Turks and the Italians. But it is even more than that. It is our traditions, everything that makes us Rhodians and Greek. It is why all our children inherit equally, even the girls, for they must be properly endowed for marriage. It is the reason why an elder brother will wait to marry himself until he has found husbands for all his sisters. It is necessary for him to be able to live comfortably with himself."

"Is that why you waited until now to marry? Because your sister had to be married first?"

"It was as good a reason as any," he muttered. "Don't make too much of it, Eleanor."

She felt the tears pricking at the back of her eyes. "How can I not? You weren't kind, Ioannis! How could you be so brutal?"

His expression was more distant than ever. "Mind your own business, *koritsi!* What passes between Mercedes and me has nothing to do with you!"

"Hasn't it?" Eleanor could only wonder at her own bravery. "Not when you are obviously in love with her, and she with you?"

He looked directly at her then. "Is that what you think? Well, I won't deny that I felt a certain attraction in that direction at one time, but there is nothing deader than last year's ashes."

"It didn't look like that to me," she persisted. "I wish you'd tell me why you're marrying *me!* Even you must be able to see that that is of some interest to me?"

He put out a hand, moving her face round towards him. "You wouldn't begin to understand," he said at length. "It's much better you shouldn't know anything about it. You will be my wife and that will have to be enough for you! Suffice it to say that if I had wanted Mercedes, I should not have let a little thing like *philotimo* hold me back!"

"But you care for her?"

"Not in any way you would know anything about. If you hadn't taken your life in your hands with that Lars of yours, you would never have known anything about her. It would be better to pretend you don't, *agapí!*"

Better for whom, Eleanor wondered. It seemed to her that disaster lay on every side, whatever she did. She had always known that Ioannis had greater experience than she with the opposite sex—no, that euphemism wouldn't do, she thought wryly. She had always known he had loved many other women and that he didn't love her at all. But she had not thought that he was still in touch with any of these past loves, let alone that one would appear out of the shades to haunt her.

She spoke again, with greater urgency than before, "Ioannis, I *have* to know! How can I marry you when you—when you want *her!*"

"I have never wanted her for my wife."

"That's not the point. I can't—I *won't* marry you—"

He gave her a pat on the cheek. "The decision isn't yours to make! Your family has agreed and that is that! Don't make difficulties where there are none!"

"No difficulty! There's every difficulty! And I won't pretend to look the other way! I won't marry you if I don't want to, and I don't think I do!"

His hand fastened about her wrist and he dragged her across the road to a car that she presumed to be his though she had never seen it before. He practically flung her into the passenger seat, glaring down at her as she nursed the wrist that he had so tightly grasped.

"You'll marry me because *I* say so! If you'd stayed at home as your grandmother told you to, you'd have saved yourself a great deal of misery, but you must always take your own way and now you'll have to put up with the results. I'm not changing my plans because you have decided to have a nervous tantrum! Nothing is changed. Tomorrow you will be my wife and then I expect to hear less about your lost independence and more about your willingness to act with the loving dignity of the traditional Greek spouse. Understand?"

She shuddered, hiding her face in her hands. "I won't do it!"

"And I won't let you go!" He laughed briefly. "Don't push me too far, Eleanor *mou!*"

His certainty sent a quiver down her spine. He didn't care how she felt at all as long as he got his own way! And he was much more determined than she—she, who had always lacked resolution when it mattered most, and who, when positive action was called for, would hesitate and lose herself in a maze of anxieties that anyone else would have ignored as having no real importance. Was it going to be the same now? Was she going to marry him because she couldn't bring herself to cross him—because it was *expected* of her?

She chewed on her lip, as uncertain as ever. "I'll marry you if I must," she began in an agonised whisper, "but I won't be your wife until—until I know where I stand—"

"Oh, Eleanor, what a fool you are! How long do you

think either of us would be content with that? You are my wife and my woman, *karthia mou,* whether you like it or not!"

She began to think of the alternatives to exchanging her vows with him in church the next day, and her spirits failed her. What would she tell her grandmother? Nothing that would cause Mrs. Barron to pay the slightest heed. She had settled in her own mind where she was going to live and she wouldn't easily be diverted from having her own way in that. Nor would her family in England support her. They would think, with a certain justice, that she had got herself into this and it was up to her to find her own way out of it.

The tears brimmed over and ran their course down her cheeks. She wiped them away angrily, knuckling her eyes until they ached with the pressure, but still she couldn't stop crying. If she wasn't careful she would really let go and sob her heart out and with it the misery of finding out that Ioannis was in love with someone else. It had been bad enough to know he didn't love her, but for him to feel the pangs of desire for Mercedes, cold and beautiful as she was, was more than Eleanor could bear.

"I thought *karthia* meant 'heart,'" she said in a drowned voice, anxious to put him at his ease because no man likes to see a woman weep and she had no wish to embarrass him. "It's a ridiculous expression when you can't possibly mean it!"

He put his arms round her, ignoring her tearful protests. So closely did he hold her, she could feel his laughter against her, and could only wonder that he could be so unfeeling.

"You do speak a few words of Greek then?" he murmured against her ear.

"I've been shopping for Grandma once or twice," she admitted. "The butcher regards her as English and that annoys her and so she sends me to get the meat while she buys the other things."

"Not a very romantic connection!" he said dryly.

"No." She sniffed, trying to ease her hand into the pocket of her jeans to find her handkerchief. "But I suppose it was nice of you to call me by any endearment when you can't feel much like it. Only, I'd rather you didn't—not just now!"

He pushed her head back against his shoulder. "Is that what you're crying about?" he asked her.

"I'm not crying!"

She could feel him laughing again at that. "My dear Eleanor, you have no means of knowing what you are to me! Would it be too much to ask of you to be a little more realistic about our marriage? What are you so afraid of? That I won't make you happy? But I assure you I will!"

With Mercedes knocking on the back door? Eleanor pushed herself away from him, marvelling that any man could be so blind. *Unrealistic?* If anyone was that, it was surely he!

"If I knew more about you—"

He restrained her from moving any further away by the simple expedient of locking his hands behind her back.

"You know all you need to know, *agapi*. If you protest any more I shall be tempted to teach you something about yourself you have yet to learn.

Marriage is unattractive to you, is it? Certainly not with me!"

She was staggered by his arrogance and by the loud beating of her heart that greeted his assertion. Her face burned with embarrassment and, if she could, she would have got out of the car and gone as far away from him as possible.

"You can't be sure of that!" she exclaimed. "It isn't true! I won't let it be true!"

"You can't go against your own nature," he pointed out, sounding so sure of himself that she winced, angered by her own weakness.

"But it's all so hopeless!" she murmured crossly. "And I won't be coerced, Ioannis! I won't!"

She was beginning to sound hysterical and she couldn't be surprised at it. She had never been more miserable in her life!

"Won't you?" She caught the menace in his very quietness and lack of fuss, and gave him a scared look. His grey-green eyes looked back at her, bright with enquiry. "I think you'll be everything I want you to be, Eleanor *mou,* even if you are a trifle reluctant at the beginning."

She felt hot and cold all over. "What makes you think that?" she asked him sourly.

"This," he said.

She tried to evade his embrace but he was much stronger than she had ever imagined and, in this instance, he was ruthlessly determined to bend her to his will.

"You're hurting me!" she cried out.

"Then stop fighting me! You are hurting yourself, as you always will when you pit your strength against mine, little one."

She stopped struggling. Indeed, she very nearly stopped breathing altogether, so intent was she on proving to him that she didn't care what he did. He would hardly want a cold, unresponsive woman in his arms, she reasoned, and would let her go as soon as he found that he couldn't arouse her in any way at all.

"Better, my love!" he commended her, a ghost of laughter at the back of his throat. "Shall I make you admit to total defeat?"

Fear tensed her muscles and shone out of her eyes. "I'm not your love!" she declared, restlessly seeking some way of escape from him. The feel of his hands through her shirt and his warm breath on her cheek was a tantalising sensation. "Ioannis, I'm not!"

He put his mouth against hers with a gentleness that threatened the last of her defenses. Her arms slipped up round his neck, her fingers burying themselves in the short hairs at the back of his head. Her carefully thought-out resistance slipped beyond her control, and with it all thought of Mercedes. Her lips parted beneath his and she gave a sob of surrender, abandoning herself wholly to his embrace.

"You'll do," he said at length. "Believe me, you'll do!"

"But as what?" she moaned.

He gave her a last kiss. "You'll have to work that one out for yourself, but understand this much, Eleanor, you're going to marry me tomorrow, and you're going to put a good face on it. You'll look eager—a little shy perhaps, but eager to be Mrs. Nikkolides! You'll answer to me if you don't!"

"And be bullied some more, I suppose!"

He ran his hand over her face, his lips twisting into a wry smile. "If you call this bullying you, it might answer very well!" He looked deep into her eyes, and was apparently satisfied by what he saw there. "Come on, my girl, it's time I took you home!"

His girl! A shadow crossed her face at the thought. What he didn't know—what he must never know!—was that she only wished she were.

"You look terrible!" Mrs. Barron told her. "What on earth have you been doing?"

"Well, that's frank anyway," Eleanor answered lightly. "I went to the Butterfly Valley."

"Ah yes, *Pentaloúdes!* After the middle of September there is nothing to see, but from June till then it can be a very pretty sight. What did you think of them?"

"Lovely!"

"It's more than you are! You look as if you'd been pulled through a bush backwards! You've no more sense than a child, Eleanor. Don't you realise that you have to look your best tomorrow. Go and wash your hair, *pedhi*, before I lose all patience with you, and then you can sit quietly beside me here and put the last touches to your dress." She gave her granddaughter a shrewd, all-encompassing glance. "I suppose I should be grateful that you have been taught to use your needle. From what I have observed there are few girls in England who have much talent in that direction!"

Meaning Sonia, Eleanor supposed, who had never been known to ply her needle on any occasion. "You're too harsh, Grandma," she said. "People cultivate different talents, that's all."

"And you're too soft!" her grandmother retorted. "I hope you mean to bring up your daughters to know how to keep a house and to make their own clothes. You never know when these things may come to be useful. Think how much easier you would have found it if you had learned how to run a house like this before you came here!"

"Would it?" Eleanor sounded so doubtful that her grandmother laughed. "Most twentieth-century girls won't be called upon to live in a folk museum like this! Why should they learn to cook on an open fire when the likelihood of their ever having to do so is remote in the extreme?"

"You will have to!"

Eleanor tried not to think about it. "I'm going to persuade Ioannis to have both houses properly modernised," she claimed.

"Are you indeed? And when are you going to begin this campaign?"

Eleanor flushed. "As soon as the cooking depends on me! That will be a campaign in itself! The disasters are fewer, but they are still disasters!"

"Never mind, child, he can see you are making an effort to learn and that pleases him. He was quite complimentary over the meal you gave him the other evening."

Eleanor remembered it was not the only thing he had been complimentary about. He had liked her dress too!

"Do you know *all* about him, Grandma?" she asked with a sigh. "Sometimes I think I don't understand him at all!"

"I know enough. Kostas knew much more, of course, because he had known his parents—the whole family! You have nothing to worry about there. He comes from good Greek stock and you should make fine, healthy children between you!"

Eleanor considered the impossibility of explaining to her grandmother that the procreation of children was not her first concern in her marriage, and decided to do as she was told and go and wash her hair instead.

The primitive aspect of the household made even this simple operation into a lengthy task, however. Eleanor put some water on to heat and went to her own room in search of one of the sachet shampoos she had brought with her from England. What, she wondered, was she going to do when she had finished that meagre supply? Then she laughed at herself for being a fool. They undoubtably had similar products for sale in every village shop in Rhodes, perhaps they even sold the same brand as the one she had brought with her. Just because the house where she was living reflected the life of a century before, there was no reason to suppose that the vast majority of Rhodians lived every bit as well as she had done back home in England!

She was flicking a comb through her wet locks when her grandmother called out to her and, still holding the comb in her hand, she went out into the courtyard to see what the older woman wanted.

"We have a visitor," Mrs. Barron said with undisguised hostility. "I am told you have already met. The *thespinis* Mercedes Dimoglou, my granddaughter Eleanor Stewart. Stewart for tonight at least; tomorrow she will have a different name!"

Mercedes stood in the gateway, her face a mask. She looked for all the world like a cat about to pounce on its prey, her body coiled for the effort.

"Did you enjoy the butterflies?" she asked in her careful English.

Eleanor nodded. "I hadn't realised you were with that busload of people. They were a very mixed group, weren't they?"

"It makes no difficulty for me. I speak most European languages and for that the firm I work for pays me well. I am not a nobody who has to be sold into marriage by her male relations, like so many others here in Rhodes!"

"But—" Eleanor began.

"You thought we were more modern? Why should you think that? You are willing to benefit from our customs yourself, aren't you?"

Eleanor felt at a loss. "My grandmother is Greek," she said weakly.

"I am Rhodian too," Mrs. Barron chimed in. "This was my brother's house since before I married and went away. Now I shall live here myself and be content to grow old amongst my own people. Why don't you sit down, Mercedes? Eleanor will make us coffee." She waved a hand at Eleanor's wet head. "Be off, girl, and get us some refreshments—and do something with your hair while you are gone! It isn't pleasant to have you dripping all over us!"

Eleanor grinned, glad to go. It would give her a few moments to herself, to grow used to the idea that Mercedes must have come for some purpose and that that purpose was probably to hurt her.

She dragged out the business of making the coffee for as long as she dared, putting out on a plate some biscuits and some cookies her grandmother had made that day. Then she carried the whole out to the courtyard, putting the tray down beside her grandmother for her to pour out at her leisure.

"I hope you will accept my granddaughter's idea of a cup of coffee," Mrs. Barron said with some humour. "I have been unable to persuade her to drink it as a Greek should, from a small cup, black and very strong, and syrupy with sugar."

Eleanor smiled at her. "I hate Greek coffee!"

Mercedes accepted her cup with a barely repressed shudder. "Is that the only thing Greek you hate?" she enquired.

Eleanor tried to ignore the malice behind the question. "I know you call it Greek coffee, but in England we call it Turkish. I always end up with a mouthful of grains, and I don't much care for sweet things anyway."

"And you, Kyria Athena, how do you like having to come back to the more limited life of the island? Were you very reluctant to leave England?"

Mrs. Barron laughed softly. "My reason for living is gone, my dear. But as we get older we all get a yen for the things we knew as children. I am well content to be back in Rhodes, and to have my granddaughter established nearby."

Mercedes slowly raised her immaculately plucked brows. Her reactions were always carefully considered and never more so than now. "But how often will she be in Rhodes, *kyria?* Does Ioannis mean to live here permanently?"

"It is possible," Mrs. Barron snapped. "What is it to you if he does?"

Mercedes raised her cup thoughtfully to her lips. "It was on that understanding that I came home in the first place. Didn't you know that? Oh yes, I was working in Athens before, doing the same job as I am here. Ioannis' sister is my closest friend—we were practically brought up together! It was Ioannis' idea that I should come home to Rhodes. He said he'd follow as soon as he had his sister wed." She turned to Eleanor, the smile on her lips quite failing to reach her eyes. "You probably don't understand *all* our customs, despite having a Greek grandmother, but we're still very old-fashioned in some ways and it's often considered necessary for a man to delay his own wedding until he has found satisfactory husbands for all his sisters. That is what we were waiting for."

"Philotimo," Eleanor said wisely. "I have heard of it."

"It has always been expected we should marry," Mercedes went on, just as if Eleanor had not spoken. "My father and Ioannis' father were partners at one time. My father is retired now, and is living in Rhodes."

"And Ioannis' father?" Eleanor couldn't resist asking.

"Is dead. He died quite suddenly last year. It was a tragedy for both our families! My father, naturally, draws a pension from the business, but he has never liked to feel that he was a millstone around Ioannis' neck. He has so many other commitments! That's why it was agreed between them that we should marry. As Ioannis' father-in-law, his position would be quite different, and I would not go to the marriage empty-handed. I have saved a handsome dowry out of my salary—better, I daresay, than yours can be?"

Mrs. Barron stirred restlessly. "My granddaughter's dowry is this house, as well as all the usual household effects. Ioannis has no cause for complaint!"

"But no money," Mercedes pointed out. "Ioannis already has one house that no one in their right mind would live in! Why should he want two?"

Why indeed? How often had Eleanor wondered that! She cast a slanting, upward look at her grandmother, expecting to see her in a fine rage, but Mrs. Barron looked merely uncomfortable.

"It is out of my hands," she said at last. "My brother, Kostas, arranged everything with Ioannis. It was none of my doing!"

Mercedes turned to Eleanor. "I came this evening because I felt so sorry for you!" she exclaimed. "To marry a man you know nothing about! It is terrible! Too terrible to contemplate! In England I am told, such a thing never happens nowadays. It would be unthinkable! You must have been shocked almost out of your mind to find yourself in such a position! But you are not married to him yet—"

In the background Hyperion, the last of Uncle Kostas' line in cocks, crowed loudly. Eleanor tried not to giggle. Really, the bird had no tact at all! It was sunset now, not sunrise, but perhaps he didn't know the difference.

130

"The wedding is tomorrow," she said out loud. She didn't say it loudly, but she sounded quite definite. "Perhaps you would like to come?"

"And see Ioannis married to another?" Mercedes gulped down the last of her coffee. "You're a fool if you think any wedding ceremony will be the end of the matter though! I haven't waited for him all this time to go empty-handed now!"

Eleanor felt an immense pity for the other girl. Knowing it would be unwelcome, she averted her face and held out her cup for her grandmother to refill for her.

"I am sorry," she murmured. "I'm sure Ioannis didn't know."

"How I felt? Of course he knew! How long do you suppose he will be faithful to an insipid English girl like yourself? Does he love you?"

"He says he wants me as his wife." Eleanor took a firmer grip on herself, dismayed because she felt a little sick—and could it be that she was angry? She was *jealous!* How could she be? Next, she would be thinking herself in love with him!

Her face was ashen as she turned back to Mercedes and met the malice in the other girl's eyes head on. "I trust Ioannis." Her voice shook painfully. "I'll always trust him. I'm sorry you've been hurt. There must have been a misunderstanding. I don't think he ever intended to marry you as you thought."

"A misunderstanding? No man does such a thing to me and gets away with it!"

Eleanor bit her lip. "That's between you and Ioannis. It has nothing to do with me!"

"No? *But I had him first!* Remember that tomorrow on your wedding day. Remember me, because I shall be there, laughing at the two of you! How will you like that? To lie in Ioannis' arms and know he is thinking of *me* and the delights we knew together! Poor Eleanor! What a shame you had to see us together this afternoon! He probably thought you'd never know—or guess! He assumes that you are too innocent to notice if your husband absents himself for hours together with his lover. Well, that's how it will be, my dear! That's how it's always been!"

Eleanor shrank back from the venom in the passionately spoken words. She had no ready answer she could make, only a silence in which she did battle with the waves of shame she felt both for Mercedes and herself.

It was left to Kyria Athena to answer for her. "My granddaughter is not so naive that she doesn't know the value of being a man's wife. Be careful, girl, or other men will leave you too. You have done enough damage to yourself, but both Eleanor and I will forget we ever heard you admit to as much. That is the least we can do for the sake of your family. You had best be gone now before Ioannis hears of your visit. If you go too far, I doubt you will find him a forgiving man! Goodnight, *thespinis* Mercedes!"

Mercedes rose to her feet. She opened her mouth to speak, changed her mind and turned abruptly on her heel.

"Goodnight, *kyria*," she answered, and was gone, her sinuous body braced against the wind from the sea.

Chapter Nine

The feel of her wedding dress swishing against her ankles as she walked brought it home to Eleanor as nothing else had done that this was her wedding day. The sun was shining as it had shone every day since she had come to Rhodes. Its warmth was reflected in the abounding fertility of the land, watered as it was by artesian wells driven by the stocky windmills that peppered the fields nearby. The sun warmed her too, bringing an eagerness to her step and an unquenchable optimism to her spirits that not even Mercedes' visit of the evening before could douse.

"Does it look nice?" she asked her grandmother, not for the first time. "As nice as you expected?"

Kyria Athena kissed her lightly on the cheek. "Nice is not the adjective I would have chosen, *koritsi,* but, yes, you look nice! And happy too! You are not as reluctant as you thought you would be perhaps?"

"It was difficult adjusting to the idea," Eleanor answered primly, not liking to admit that it was not adjusting to the notion of being married to Ioannis that had been difficult, but that she should do so easily, without the love she had always thought would be essential to tempt her out of her single state. "I prefer to think for myself, you see. I always shall!"

"That should be quite satisfactory as long as your thinking reflects that of Ioannis," her grandmother said wryly. "It won't get you very far if it doesn't!"

"Oh, I don't know," Eleanor claimed, "Ioannis isn't as old-fashioned as all that!"

"You think not? He is a man, my child. Very much a man! If one marries such a man one has much to be thankful for in the flowering of one's own womanhood, but one has to pay the price too. Ioannis won't just dominate you sexually, he'll dominate your whole life. And quite right too! What woman would have it any other way?"

Not her, not if she could have his love too! Eleanor looked down at her dress, tracing the embroidered motif at the neck with her fingers.

"What did you think of Mercedes?" she asked suddenly.

"A vulgar individual," Mrs. Barron responded immediately. "She has a certain attraction, but is not what

I would describe as marriageable material. You can be sure that is what Ioannis has decided too! There is no need for you ever to see her again, my dear, if that is what is worrying you."

Eleanor attempted a halfhearted smile. "She has a way of turning up whether I like it or not," she said.

"And how long do you think Ioannis will put up with such behaviour?"

The caustic note in her grandmother's voice made Eleanor laugh, but then the Kyria Athena didn't know what Mercedes did, that Ioannis had been in love with Mercedes and probably still was, and that he wasn't in love with Eleanor at all. There was a physical attraction between them that she had already found out was usless for her to deny, but that was very little on which to build the whole edifice of a successful marriage.

"Should I put my gloves on or not?" she enquired, changing the subject with an abruptness that brought her grandmother's concerned gaze to her face. "I've never worn long gloves before and I'm rather awkward with them."

Mrs. Barron sighed. "I can't think how you modern young girls would have managed in my day! We wore gloves as a matter of course and, believe me, in a place like London they were extremely difficult to keep clean and fresh. I was forever washing gloves and easing them onto glove-stretchers when they were wet and clammy! Manmade fabrics are a great blessing!"

"I never wear gloves at all except on a very cold day. Supposing I put these on and can't get them off again in church?"

"You'd better carry them," her grandmother decided

with resignation. "You can carry them in one hand and the bouquet Ioannis has sent for you in the other."

Eleanor flushed. It was the first she had heard about Ioannis having sent her flowers. "What has he sent?" she asked.

"Roses. What else? We are in Rhodes, my dear." She glanced at Eleanor's eager face. "They're on the table in your room if you want to see them, only, *please*, don't disturb them, or get yourself in a mess while I'm changing my dress! I don't like to let you out of my sight for a single moment, knowing what you can do to yourself in no time at all! If you must do something, stand up while you're doing it! I will not have you crushing that skirt by sitting on it! Is that clear?"

"Loud and clear," Eleanor teased her. "I'll be very, very careful, I promise you!"

"See that you are!" her grandmother retorted testily. "You're looking lovely, my dear, and I'd like to see Ioannis see you that way! That would give Mercedes something to think about!"

Eleanor didn't think Mercedes would even notice what anyone else was looking like, so self-absorbed did she think that young lady to be, but there was no point in telling her grandmother that. Instead, she put an affectionate hand on her shoulder and smiled at her.

"Grandma, I haven't thanked you—for the dress and for everything—"

"There's no need, child. One shouldn't have favourites, but you were always my favourite grandchild! In you, I can see a lot of myself as I was at your age. I, too, found my whole world in my husband. Be happy in your marriage, as I was in mine! I ask nothing more for you than that!"

She bustled away to change her own dress just as the cock crowed several times. She clicked her tongue and smiled over her shoulder at Eleanor.

"We shall have to get that bird some pullets to look after! What good is a rooster on his own except for the pot and he is far too handsome for such a fate! I shall talk to Ioannis about it some time. We could share the eggs and save poor Hyperion from becoming neurotic at the same time!"

"If you ask me, he's already round the bend," Eleanor answered. "He doesn't even know the time of day. I'm not sure he isn't vicious too."

Mrs. Barron wasn't put off one bit. "Let's hope Ioannis is more sympathetic than you are. Don't you want some nice, fresh eggs for your table?"

Eleanor laughed. "Oh, you'll find Ioannis sympathetic all right," she said. "He shares the same name after all—and other characteristics too!" she added reflectively.

Her grandmother's earthy laughter made her blush. "He does more than crow!" the older woman chuckled. "You'll find out!"

Eleanor raised an eyebrow with a dignified air. "He may find out a thing or two also!"

But her grandmother only laughed the more heartily and disappeared into her room, her shoulders shaking with merriment. Left alone, Eleanor shook her fist at the bright-eyed cockerel that had come right up to the entrance to the courtyard in search of food and to mock her with his crowing when none was forthcoming.

"What happened to your wives, Hyperion?" she mocked him in her turn. "Did they leave you because you promised the sun and only gave them the darkness of night? You should learn the difference between the dawn and the sunset!"

"Do you know the difference, *yinéka mou?*"

She turned, startled, and saw that Ioannis had come up behind the bird and was leaning against the doorjamb, his arms crossed over his chest. He was dressed in a sober, slate-grey suit with a flowered shirt that was matched exactly by his tie. He looked unbelievably handsome.

"You shouldn't be here!" she shot at him. "It's incredibly unlucky for you to see me in my wedding dress before we meet in church!"

He looked amused. "An English superstition? I didn't know you indulged in such fancies. You forget that the eye of the sun has been on you all morning, seeking you out to tell you how lovely you are looking. Come close, Eleanor, and let me look at you properly."

She did so, standing shyly before him, her fingers once again finding the embroidered motif at her neck. "Isn't it unlucky in Greece?" she asked him.

"Nothing is unlucky between us!" He unwound himself and took a step towards her, his fingers meeting hers on her bodice and pulling hers away. "Are you going to pretend that isn't an I intermingled with the E on this dress too?"

His eyes were as bright as the rooster's. Eleanor's fell before them. "Grandma—"

"She embroiders beautifully, but those are not her

stitches," he interrupted her. "Your grandmother has the sight of an old woman and her work is not as perfect as it once was."

"She designed the motif," Eleanor went on doggedly. "She would have been hurt if I had changed it in any way."

He bent his head to look at it more closely. "So would I have been, *agapí mou*. I like it as it is!" He traced the pattern with his forefinger. "The roses of Rhodes, with the stag and the doe, and you and me. Have you seen the roses I sent you?"

"They're in my room. Th—thank you, Ioannis." Annoyed with herself for stammering, she turned scarlet under his amused eyes and, taking to her heels, fled from him and the rooster, running harder as the bird opened his beak to crow once more.

She arrived breathless in her room and stood for a moment, heart pounding, by the door, half-hoping that Ioannis would leave and more than half-hoping he wouldn't. She was being ridiculous of course, flattening herself against the wall so that he wouldn't see that she was looking out of the open door *at him!* When she felt a little calmer she would go out to him again—carrying the roses he had brought her. *The roses!* She hadn't even glanced at them!

She made a mad dash over to the table and came to a full stop in front of them, her eyes starting out of her head. They were beautiful! The most beautiful roses she had ever seen, each one hand-picked and stripped of its thorns, a perfect example of its kind. They were in two colours, a soft cream and a coral pink, shaded into one another by the careful choice of each bloom. They were tied with a ribbon that exactly matched the thread of the embroidery on her dress.

She came out of the room more slowly, carrying the roses over her arm. She had no words left with which she could thank Ioannis again for them. Instead, she silently held them out to him, her eyes filling with tears.

"They become you very well," he said.

"Do they?" She blinked. "I'm glad you think so. I thought you might be wishing you had chosen another flower—one you knew better, that you *liked* better? Only—" She broke off, unable to continue.

"Only what?" he prompted her.

"I hope you'll come to like roses too!" she said in a rush. "They're more—more *lasting* than some other flowers!"

"True." He sounded amused again and she thought she would never forgive him for that, at a moment when she was trying to tell something that was important to them both. "Don't fret, sweetheart," he said more gently. "For us, roses are the ideal flower. They symbolise both England and Rhodes. What could be more suitable?"

"I think English roses are red," she said flatly.

But he shook his head, far more sure of his facts than she was. "There were two roses," he told her. "The red rose of Lancashire, the white rose of York. When they were united by Henry VII's marriage to Elizabeth, the rose became a double one, combining the two colours to make a pink. I have seen it on a baptismal font in England that was put up in early Tudor times."

"Have you?" She held the roses closer to her. "I didn't know you'd been to England."

"There is a great deal you don't know about me."

She cast anxious eyes over his face, seeking an understanding she had not so far received from him. " I don't know anything about you!" she exclaimed.

He smiled at that, pulling her close against him. "You will have plenty of time to find out! Come, kiss me for the roses, and I'll leave you to get ready for the ceremony in peace."

"Eleanor!"

Her grandmother's shriek of dismay made Eleanor wince away from him and between them they dropped the roses onto the *chocklaki* floor. With a gasp of dismay, Eleanor sank to her knees to retrieve them, but he was there before her, his lips against her cheeks, quivering with laughter as she tried to avoid his kiss.

"Eleanor, you must be more careful! You will stain your dress!" Kyria Athena moaned. "Make her get up, Ioannis! It is intolerable that she can't stand still for two minutes!"

Ioannis held out a gallant hand, his eyes on Eleanor's chagrined features. "I rather like to have her at my feet," he responded dryly. "We have been discussing roses, Kyria Athena. Your granddaughter thought I might prefer another flower. You will have to tell her it was I who chose the rose, and I who chose the colour too, with which she has embroidered my chosen symbol on her dress! Arise, Eleanor, and haste you to the church! I shall be waiting for you there!"

He was gone while she was still scrambling to her

feet, the precious roses held lovingly in her arms. She gazed down at them, touching the smoothness of their creamy petals, her eyes full of dreams she knew could never be realised.

The church came as a surprise to Eleanor. She didn't know what she had been expecting, but it had been nothing like the golden lit basilica into which she stepped from the hot sun outside. The altar was hidden from her by the *iconostasis*, a screen of icons in the centre of which were some double doors through which the priest, gloriously robed in cloth of gold, came and went. The chandeliers shone like drops of diamonds and they, too, were decorated with icons, representations of all the more famous saints of the eastern Church.

She took her place beside Ioannis and the bouquet of roses was taken away from her. She didn't dare look to either side, but kept her eyes on the patterned marble floor, trying to believe that it was true she was being married to the man beside her. It didn't feel real at all. It felt as though she had wandered into a foreign world where nothing made sense and nothing was likely to do so. Her hand was bound to Ioannis' with ribbons, and garlands of flowers were held over their heads, crowning them with happiness. Afterwards, they followed the priests in a complete circle, representing the unbreakable union into which they had entered, the circle of eternity that has no beginning and no end. The priest, his long hair hanging down his back, held three lighted candles in one hand, symbolising the Trinity, and two in his other, symbolising the Old and the New Covenants. He spoke only in Greek, carefully prompting Eleanor in her responses, but little seemed to be required of her except to follow Ioannis' lead and to lose herself in the wealth of colour and sound that whirled about her.

When it was over, they emerged into the sunshine again, and the villagers pressed round them, exchanging warm embraces and admiring Eleanor's dress and the bouquet of roses that was somehow back in her arms. She had nothing to say to these strangers for, even if she had had enough Greek to speak to them, she would have been too overcome to mutter more than a few words. It was better left to Ioannis who seemed quite untouched by the beauty of the Greek wedding ceremony, and her grandmother who had found her tongue with a vengeance and was bridling with pleasure and excitement just as if it had been her own wedding.

"What happens now?" Eleanor asked Ioannis in an undertone, narrowly escaping another scented embrace from a large-bosomed woman who had wept all over her once already.

"What do you want to happen?"

She blinked. "Are they all coming home with us?"

"Do you mind? They will sing and dance all night if we let them. Your grandmother will enjoy that, but will you?"

She nodded almost eagerly. *It would solve a lot of problems,* she thought. "I like to watch the dancing," she said. "Your Greek music is lovely to listen to! Will the women dance this time too?"

"Very likely. Will you dance with me?"

She couldn't quite bring herself to look at him. "I don't know the steps," she said.

"I could teach you."

But she shook her head. "I expect I'll be too busy helping Grandma with the refreshments. Her arthritis hurts her more when she gets tired."

His eyes gleamed with mockery. "She looks as agile as a mountain goat right now!"

"Yes, but she's excited *now*," Eleanor explained. "But that won't last all night!"

He bent his head to hers. "Excuses won't serve you very well tonight, Eleanor *mou*. Are you ready to go?"

She hadn't realised that they were to lead the procession home. How different it all would have been at home in England, she thought. There would have been the grey stone parish church with its familiar stained glass windows and organ music, and afterwards there would have been cars to transport everyone to the reception, no matter how short the distance. Here, everything was strange to her. The church with its stiff, stern-faced saints and plain glass windows, the music that was wholly vocal and with an eastern quality that came directly from the ancient synagogues of Israel, long before the birth of Christianity. And strangest of all was Ioannis, who had married her without love and who thought it quite an ordinary thing to do. How could he, she wondered, when his heart was filled with someone else's image? Yet the choice had been his, more his than it had ever been hers!

The road was rough and uneven beneath her feet as they made their way through the narrow streets of the village and took the turning down to the sea from which the track that served their two houses branched off. She could feel the loose pebbles through the thin soles of her fabric shoes. Once or twice, she was afraid she might stumble and she put a hand on Ioannis' arm to steady herself, clutching the roses closer against her.

"English roses don't always smell nowadays," she told him solemnly. "They were made more and more perfect to look at, but their scent suffered accordingly. I wonder why that didn't happen in Rhodes?"

"We have the sun."

The answer caught her unawares, undermining the air of confidence she had spent so long acquiring. That this was the island of roses and the sun, she was no longer in doubt. It was the sun that made the colours of the island so intense they almost hurt, the sea a bold splash of inky blue, the leaves of the trees a shimmering green that danced in the hot rays from above. The sun, too, had darkened her own skin and burnished her hair, and she felt its warmth like a caress, and had thought of Ioannis, whose middle name was Hyperion and who might well have been another aspect of the Titan Sun.

"If English roses were brought here, would their scent improve?" she wondered aloud.

The look he gave her was very intimate, almost as though he could read her thoughts and was amused by them.

"I think so," he said. "I think an English rose may do so too, don't you?"

He could only have been talking about herself! She glanced uncertainly back at him, smiling a little.

"I'll try," she said. "I promise you I'll try."

"I know you will." His smile mocked her, though it was gently done. "Now you've made your vows both in English and in Greek, *agapí,* and all the gods will stand witness to that if you are ever tempted to change your mind!"

"Which gods?" she retorted. "Yours or mine?"

"Are they so different? I think not. Their names make a familiar list: Helios, Rodos, Aphrodite, Apollo, Artemis, Athena, Poseidon, the lord of the sea, and Zeus, the king of the gods. Beware, lest they should ever come to bear witness against you, Eleanor, *yinéka mou!* They gave you to me, and what I have, I hold!"

She was fascinated by the roll of names that fell so easily from his lips. "I don't believe in your gods!" she denied.

He was amused. "You take them too seriously to believe in them," he agreed, "but one day they will come up behind you and take you unawares. They are only the personifications of qualities known to all men."

She thought that might be true. She didn't believe in them—of course she didn't believe in them!—but since coming to Rhodes she had been aware of their shadows moving in the distance, just out of sight, where she couldn't definitely verify their being, but couldn't deny them entirely either.

She could hear her grandmother talking just behind her and began to consider the name she had been given by her parents. It was a good, safe subject to think about, she told herself, safer than anything else that occurred to her, for all other subjects seemed to lead back to Ioannis. Had her grandmother received the quality of wisdom along with the name Athena? Eleanor thought perhaps she had. Since she had got to know her better in these last few days, she had often thought her grandmother wise in the ways of life and understanding in her relations with others. Perhaps Athena, the goddess, had served her well after all.

Her grandmother raised her voice to catch her attention. "Eleanor, I did tell you I am staying with my cousin for the next few days?"

Eleanor was astonished. "No." She dropped her arm from Ioannis' arm and turned to face Mrs. Barron. "Why? I thought nothing was ever going to shift you from that house again?"

Her grandmother looked positively gleeful. "You won't want me there on your honeymoon, child! You and Ioannis need a few days to yourselves."

It was the last thing Eleanor wanted! She put out a hand to Ioannis, seeking his support, but he only shook his head at her.

"I haven't much holiday left," he said, "and then we shall have to go back to Athens."

"*Athens?*"

"Where I work, my sweet. Now I have a wife to support, it's more important than ever that I should make a success of the firm I run. Don't you think so?"

"But—*Athens?* I thought you were a Rhodian?"

"I am, but I live most of my time in Athens. I come here whenever I can, and you will come with me, but we can't stay here all the year round. I thought you understood that?"

"No," Eleanor responded blankly. She thought about it for a moment. "Then this house is your holiday home?" Anger stirred within her breast. "What have I been doing, struggling to learn how to keep such a house going, very much against my inclination, I may say, when we're only going to be here a few weeks in every year?"

His hand found the small of her back and drew her close against him. "To please me?" he suggested on a note so intimate it sounded practically indecent to her.

"Certainly not!" she declared. "Oh, I do think you might have told me! I've never been to Athens! How do I know I'm going to like it any better than here?" She lifted belligerent eyes to his. "It would serve you right if I refused to budge out of my own house!"

He laughed, completely confident that he could make her change her mind. "My dear girl, your house became my house a few moments ago, just as you became mine! Shall we lead our friends inside to help us celebrate that fact, or would you rather I sent them away?"

And what gossip that would cause! Defeated, Eleanor lifted her chin proudly and cast a dazzling smile over the waiting villagers.

"Of course you must invite them in! What else did they come for? But it isn't the end of the matter, Ioannis, don't think that! I may have married you but I'm not yet your wife, and it will take more than crowing to make me so!"

"I think I shall manage." He patted her cheek, his smile cynical and not very kind. "I enjoy most challenges, *agapí*, and I shall enjoy this one more than most! Will you?"

She almost missed her footing altogether, but she

was too proud to show him how the thrust had gone home. Carefully, she made her face a blank, seeking the only way she could think of to have her revenge and finding it.

"If you live in Athens, why did you send Mercedes back to Rhodes?" she hissed at him, taking his proffered hand by putting her own down flat on top of his.

"Because I live in Athens," he said.

It told her nothing and it wasn't meant to. Her rage—or was it quite another emotion?—rose to a dangerous level. She stepped into the courtyard of his house before him, feeling as though she were stepping off the brow of a volcano into the boiling, troubled depths that might explode at any moment. But the shock of what she saw there was as effective as an ice-cold bucket of water thrown over her head. Chaos reigned, the tables and chairs thrown from one place to another, and the carefully assembled food spilt all over the *chocklaki* floor. Hatred and malice were evident everywhere, and she shivered, conscious that it had been directed at her, and her alone.

"Why? Ioannis, why?" she whispered.

His face was cast in a mould of tragic anger that she felt was also meant for her. How could he blame her? But it seemed he did. He turned on his heel and left her alone in the middle of the ruins of the courtyard, saying something in Greek to the assembled, astonished guests. Eleanor tried to follow him, but he would have none of it.

"Go back and clean the place up!" he commanded her.

"But, Ioannis, what about—"

"Eleanor, do as you're told! Won't you ever learn to leave well enough alone? Your grandmother will cope with everything else, but I expect this house to be habitable by the time I come back, and to find you in it waiting for me! Is that clear enough for you?"

She shivered and nodded, her eyes pricking with tears. "It isn't my fault!" she almost sobbed.

"Nobody said it was!" He looked away from her, his features stiff and unyielding. "I shan't be long so you haven't much time, *yinéka mou!* You'd best get on with it!"

Yinéka mou! My woman! *His* woman! What a laugh that was! For Eleanor knew as well as everybody else did who had perpetrated this outrage to ruin her wedding day. It was obviously and undoubtedly the work of Mercedes Dimoglou, the love of his life, and the only woman in the whole world Eleanor had ever hated!

150

Chapter Ten

Left alone, Eleanor gave way to tears. The receding voices of the villagers made her feel more lonely than ever. They might have stayed—her grandmother might even have suggested it to them and they could all have cleared up the mess together and then gone on to have the party just the same. But nobody had thought of that. Appalled, they had whispered together and had faded away, leaving her by herself to face up to the disastrous beginning of her marriage as best she could.

She didn't even know where to begin to restore order from the chaotic mess that surrounded her. She removed her wedding dress with nerveless fingers, folding it with tissue paper and burying it at the bottom of the chest that held her clothes and which somebody had brought across from the other house. Then she turned her attention to picking up the chairs, disposing of those which were damaged beyond repair and placing the others round the walls of the courtyard well out of the way.

There was no hope for any of the food. Eleanor stared down at it, her grief getting the better of her. Her grandmother had gone to so much trouble for her and she hadn't even realised it at the time. And now it was all wasted, together with the wine and bottles of lemonade Ioannis had provided for the feast. All that remained was squalor and broken glass.

She fetched a broom from inside the house, one of the type she had never learned to manage with any positive results, and swung it with a will over the *chocklaki* floor. Some of the debris obligingly heaped up into a pile in the centre of the courtyard, the rest of it fell between the smoothed-off pebbles and refused to budge no matter what she did.

For once she was pleased to see Hyperion, the rooster, come stalking into the courtyard as if he owned it, his bright eye watching her every movement.

"Okay, eat!" she bade him. "I don't see why you shouldn't benefit as no one else will. You can begin over there, you stupid bird!"

Hyperion was nothing if not obliging. He sampled all the delicacies as if they were no more than his due, relishing the mixture of cake and wine and stuffing it down into his overloaded crop as fast as he possibly could.

Eleanor stood and watched him, hands on hips, the tears pouring down her face. It was hard not to see the fiasco as symbolic of her whole future. Mercedes had won! She had pulled down the bridge Eleanor and Ioannis had been tentatively building towards each other with a brutality that Eleanor was sure had effectively killed any burgeoning affection between them once and for all.

"Enjoying yourself?" she asked Hyperion with a sarcasm that was completely lost on the bird. "Have some more!"

The cock staggered across the courtyard, his gait rather less secure than when he had entered. He tried desperately to peck his way through another cake, but his movements became less and less controlled.

"You're drunk!" Eleanor accused him.

The rooster hung his head and his beak gaped. He looked very sick indeed. "You pea-brained bird! What am I to do with you?"

Hyperion's eye refused to focus and he reeled dangerously on the spot where he stood. Was it possible, Eleanor wondered, that such a little alcohol could induce such a state in a cock like Hyperion?

"I suppose I shall have to put you to bed as well as everything else!" she sighed, approaching him with caution lest he should suddenly recover and peck her for her pains.

Hyperion, however, made no protest at all. She picked him up bodily and deposited him on a nest of leaves and grass she scratched up for him just inside the entrance to the courtyard, and he let her do it, his resistance to the human race completely gone. He lay where she put him, his head falling forward and his eyes half-closed.

"Poor symbol of the sun," Eleanor cooed at him. "You'd better sleep it off before your namesake sees you! You'll have a fine headache in the morning as it is, without his wringing your neck for letting the side down!"

"What's the matter with him?" Ioannis' voice asked her, giving her such a fright that she toppled over backwards and sat there on the floor, trying to still the frantic thumping of her pulses.

"He's drunk. The wine went to what he's pleased to call his head. Bird-brained indeed!" She crossed her legs in front of her, sure that her face was dirty and her hair standing on end. "Where did you spring from? I didn't hear you coming! You could have whistled or something! I hate being made to feel a fool!"

He stood where he was, looking down at her. "Now why should you feel a fool?" he wondered aloud.

"You know why! The place still looks a mess—and I can't help it! And the wine has stained the floor and I don't think it will ever come off. And I know you think it's all my fault, but it *isn't!* I wouldn't have had it happen, not for anything!" And to complete her humiliation she started to cry again, with great, gulping sobs that hurt her somewhere in the chest and didn't make her feel any better at all.

"It isn't the end of the world," he said.

"*It is!*" Her tears came all the faster and she rubbed

154

them away with her hands, uncaring that by doing so she was both smearing her makeup, or what remained of it, and daubing herself with the dirt from the grass and leaves she had pushed together into a nest for Hyperion.

"It's unfortunate, but it's nothing to weep about, Eleanor." He sounded distant and awkward and not at all sympathetic. "Pull yourself together, *agapí,* and stop making a scene about nothing!"

"Nothing?" She leaped to her feet, drawing herself up to her full height. She was still an inch or two shorter than her husband and, for the first time, that mattered to her! She wanted to look down her nose at him for a change! To make him feel as small as he did her! "If you feel like that, you can clean it up yourself!" she stormed at him. "And I'll stand here and watch you do it!"

"Well, well," he said, surprised by her fury, a quiver of laughter beginning to surface in his voice, "you're determined to play the shrew, are you? How much of it is real, and how much a game you're playing, little Eleanor? Not that it matters either way, my sweet. Tonight I'm going to make a woman of you, however ill-done you feel yourself to be, and you can start by playing the part of wife by cleaning the house and getting your husband something to eat for his supper!"

She flew at him, arms flailing, set on wiping the smile off his lips and imposing her will on him as completely as he had more than once imposed his on her.

"English wives decide for themselves what to do! And they don't stand for being humiliated by their husband's mistresses either! *English*—"

He clipped her hands to her sides, effectively restraining her from doing him any physical violence with an ease that both humiliated her and yet, in some peculiar way, pleased her too.

"English wives are women like any others," he said flatly. "It won't help to take it out on me, Eleanor *mou*. It was my wedding too!"

The fight went out of her, replaced by a despair that swelled like a balloon within her. She was afraid that if she didn't maintain her anger with him she would start crying again, and then what would he think of her? She gave him a covert glance from beneath wet eyelashes and looked hastily away again. She knew as surely as if he had told her that he was thinking of Mercedes again and not of her at all.

"Why don't you go to her?" she said, as bitter as gall.

"She is not my wife. You are that! You had better begin to play the part before I take you up on your suggestion, because my patience is almost at an end! It's a dangerous game you're playing, to defy me today of all days!"

Eleanor was tempted to climb down and to pick up the broom again, but pride wouldn't let her. Why should it always be she who was expected to give way?

"Then go to her! I'm not stopping you!" she spat at him.

"Not physically," he agreed, as cold as she was overheated. "But the fact of you prevents me from leaving you tonight. You're my wife and I mean to keep the vows I made to you today in church—"

"I'm not your wife yet!" Her voice shook with fear and her eyes were wide. She was afraid of him, and yet not afraid. She was curious too, and there was a need inside her that only he could fulfill, and she was afraid that he would know about that as well and would relish the triumph that lay so easily in his grasp.

He let go her wrists, a tight smile twisting his lips into the semblance of humour. "You will be! I mean to have you, my Eleanor, flesh of my flesh, bone of my bone! How it will be is up to you, but have you I will. Make up your mind to it, you'll not escape me. Tonight is mine, *yinéka mou!* If you want it to be, it can be yours too, but willing or reluctant, tonight you are my wedded bride and I am going to take you for my own!"

Breathing heavily, she searched his face to see if he was serious. She was left in no doubt that he meant every word of it. She uttered a gasping sob and twisted away from him, picking up the broom and sweeping the yard as if her life depended on it. Her efforts were little more successful than they had been before and Ioannis silently held out his hand and took the broom from her.

"You get us something to eat," he said wearily, "and I'll finish out here." He smiled at her as she relinquished the broom to him and, for the first time, she thought she read something very like sympathy for her in his eyes. "We could go out," he added, "but, to tell the truth, I'm tired of other people The gossip will be bad enough tomorrow, today it would be unbearable!"

She blinked at him. "The gossip?"

"Women always talk, my dear! This little episode will travel the length and breadth of the island quicker than we could go by car! But, if you think you could stand it, I'll take you into Rhodes Town and we could dine in Mandraki harbour. How does that suit my lady?"

It didn't suit her at all. "And have everyone staring

at us?" she protested. "No, thank you very much! Besides—"

He was making a far better job of sweeping up than she had been able to do, she noticed bleakly. He had a way of using the brush that didn't make the dust fly and his long sweeping motions seemed to pick up every scrap of the debris that had fallen between the polished pebbles.

"Besides?" he prompted her.

"What if we were to bump into Mercedes?" Her tongue felt stiff in her mouth as she formed the words and the flood of tears came very close again, making her wish she had said something else, something that preferably would have diverted his attention away from herself and the comparison he must be making between herself and Mercedes.

"Eleanor, if you're wise, you'll never let me hear her name on your lips again! Mercedes will answer to me for what she has done and not to you. Forget her! She can only hurt you if you allow her to, and you have better things to do with your time than that!" He smiled slowly and very gently, his eyes on her lips and the swell of her breast beneath her bodice. "You have a husband to please, *agapí mou,* and a promise to fulfill! Think about that for a change!"

She turned away from him quickly, determined not to take his advice. The fire had burned low in the grate and she poked it vigorously, hoping to restore it to life before it went out completely. Her fingers all felt like thumbs and she found it difficult to concentrate on making a dish edible enough for them to share. Her grandmother had left some *tzatziki* ready-prepared for her. Eleanor tried a little of the yogurt dip, flavoured with cucumber and garlic, on a spoon and found it good. There were eggs too and some prawns, enough for her to make an omelette at least, and a whole bottle of wine that had escaped the wholesale destruction of its fellows. Was that going to be enough for Ioannis? She devoutly hoped so!

In the end it was he who set the table for her, and he who beat up the eggs for the omelette and shelled the prawns with quick, neat movements that she could never emulate.

"The fire looks a poor thing," he remarked.

"It won't burn up for me," she sighed. "I'll give it another poke—" But she never finished her sentence. Strong hands turned her to face him, holding her close against his chest.

"I'll do it!" He kissed her cheek. "Why don't you get ready for bed?"

"For bed?" She sounded as though she had never heard of anyone going to bed before and wished she could behave in a more dignified and less ridiculous fashion. "I'm going to bed in my own house! All—all my things are still there—and—and I prefer—"

"I prefer that you share my bed," he cut her off. "Go and wash your face, *agapí mou,* my little love, and by that time I'll have prepared something fit for us to eat!"

She went into her own courtyard and sat down on her grandmother's rocking chair, trying to think what she should do next. In a little while, she got up again and washed herself, brushing her hair until it shone, and reluctantly giving up the idea of having anything to eat that night. When she had finished, she shut herself into the room she had used ever since her grandmother's arrival, locking the door, a feat which hurt her fingers, and leaning against it until she could be sure that Ioannis was not coming after her.

The steps up to the platform which held her mattress squeaked familiarly as she mounted the steep steps and lay down shivering under the coverlet. She had wanted to be alone, but Ioannis didn't appear to have noticed her defection at all. Perhaps he didn't care? Perhaps he would take her at her word and go out to find Mercedes? Well, she wished him joy of her!

The door crashed open, the old wood round the lock splintering and tearing away from the jamb. Eleanor took a deep breath, waiting for what he would do next. She was not left long in doubt. He took a standing jump onto the platform beside her, reaching down for her and slinging her across his shoulder as easily as if she had been the coverlet she hugged closely against her.

"Ioannis, I'm not coming!" she pleaded. She kicked out at him, but his grip on her was too secure for her to do him any damage. "Let me go!"

He laughed, a loud, masculine sound that sounded very like a crow of triumph. "I warned you, Eleanor. Willing or not, you're sharing my bed tonight!"

"But I haven't had anything to eat!"

"I thought you'd decided you weren't hungry." He swung her round his body until he was holding her across his chest. "I put it down to bridal nerves and ate your share as well as my own! Come, *yinéka mou,* give me the victory and admit you want me just as much as I want you?"

Bride of the sun! The words came unbidden into her

mind and she tasted the first beginnings of her defeat. She buried her fingers in his hair and shuddered against him, the beat of her heart taking on a new rhythm.

"Are you so very reluctant, my little Eleanor?" he whispered in her ear.

She didn't answer him. She couldn't. She could only marvel at the ease with which he carried her across the courtyard and out of her grandmother's house and into his own. Her hands clutched his as he lowered her onto the bridal bed, and, dousing the lights, eased his long frame down beside her. His kisses were gentle at first, comforting her and coaxing her into giving him the response he sought, a response she was finding it increasingly hard to deny him. Then, as his embrace took on a new dimension, the tension within her broke and her body arched against his in complete surrender.

"Eleanor, my bride, *yinéka mou, s'agapo para poli, agapí mou!*"

She didn't know what the words meant, nor did she care. They sounded nice against her throat and better than any words she had ever heard before. "I love you too," she said. But she didn't say it aloud. She said it in her heart in that liquid moment when the whole world turned to gold.

She was alone when she awoke. For a while she couldn't believe that he had gone out without her, and without a word. It wasn't fair to have left her! He must have known how great her need for him was and how much she would have given to have woken in his arms to be reassured that it had not all been a dream, that she was indeed his wife.

She sprang out of bed, hurtling down the steps and out into the courtyard in case he should be there. It was as empty as the house. The blank misery that hit her shocked her deeply. There was no use in pretending to herself any longer. She was fathoms deep in love with him and she didn't think she was ever going to recover from it.

There were signs of him everywhere. She noticed with a warmth that bewildered her that he had cleared away the dishes from his meal the evening before, but had left the crumbs and the dregs of coffee from his hastily taken breakfast. So, he had left in a hurry, she decided, but where?

The answer was not long in coming to her. An opened letter had been left beneath his cup, unfolded and spread out so that she could read it if she wanted to do so. She picked it up and glanced at it, but it was in Greek and totally unintelligible to her. Only the signature made sense. She would have recognised it in any script, she thought bitterly. It was Mercedes who had written the letter and it was to Mercedes he had gone, despite all that had gone before.

Disbelief was followed by an agonising grief. Eleanor sat at the table where *he* had sat and tried to find something in her situation with which to reassure herself. She picked up Mercedes' letter again and turned it over, surprised to see that a few words in English had been hastily scrawled across the back.

Eleanor, she read, *this came and I have gone to answer it in person. You were asleep or I would have told you about it before I went. Ioannis.*

It confirmed all her worse fears. She had told him to go to Mercedes and now he had! But what was she going to do? One thing was certain: she couldn't sit here, immobilised. She had to do something, *anything,* that would help her get through these first few hours and come to terms with herself.

She would go to her grandmother!

As soon as she thought of it, she knew it was the only answer. Kyria Athena would offer her some of the wisdom she needed, and she would listen and would feel better, and then, and only then, would she be able to face the truth about herself and Ioannis.

She dressed slowly, aware of a hollow feeling in her middle that she had no intention of giving way to. It never occurred to her that she might be hungry. The mere thought of making herself some breakfast revolted her. She would go without. It would be difficult enough to find out where her grandmother was staying and to explain to her why she had come, but she was the one person in the world who would understand. Funny that, for, until the last few days, she would never have thought of her grandmother in that light, but now she was sure that she would tell her what to do and that her advice would be good.

When she had finished dressing, Hyperion began to crow, a strained, uncertain note that at another time would have amused her. He was a sad sight to see, his feathers ruffled and awry and his usually scarlet comb a pale purple and flopping over one side of his face into his eye.

"Poor bird," Eleanor greeted him. "Still feeling

seedy? Never mind, Grandma has it in mind to get some wives for you and then you won't feel the need to paint the town red at nights!" She surveyed him gloomily, reflecting he was the only one who had celebrated her wedding in any style at all.

Her grandmother was easier to find than Eleanor had expected, but not at all pleased to see her.

"Come in, child," she said from deep inside her cousin's kitchen, "if you must! Does Ioannis know you're here?"

Eleanor shook her head. "I had to talk to you," she began.

"*Now?*" Mrs. Barron sounded far from pleased. "It isn't convenient now, my dear. Melanie and I are going out for the day. We're going to Lindos to see some other relations—"

"Please, Grandma. Please may I come with you to Lindos? I won't be any bother, only I can't stay at home by myself. I can't."

"By yourself?" She had her grandmother's full attention now. "Come in, girl. It's time you met your cousin Melanie anyway. She would have met you yesterday, but, well, the less said about that the better!"

Eleanor recognised Melanie at once as the scented bosomy embrace she had tried to avoid several times the day before. It was odd to think she had Greek relations, that however distantly she and this stout black-clad woman shared some of the same blood and perhaps even more than that.

Eleanor shook hands with her, exchanged a timid

greeting in Greek, and admired the ancient wooden icon that held the place of honour in the kitchen and before which two red sanctuary lights burned. Then, duty done, she turned back to her grandmother.

"It's about yesterday—in a way. It's about Mercedes at least. Ioannis had a letter from her this morning—and he's gone to her. I told him to go—and he went!"

"*Gone?* Gone for good?"

Eleanor threaded her fingers together, hoping she wasn't going to cry again. "I don't know. He left a note saying he had gone to Mercedes before I woke up. How should I know if and when he's coming back. I only knew I wasn't going to stay there, twiddling my thumbs until he did!"

"I see. And what has he to say to this Mercedes woman?"

Eleanor hung her head. "He's in love with her!" she burst out. "Not even yesterday has changed that! Oh Grandma, he loves *her,* and I can't bear it!"

"You may be wrong, child?"

Silently, Eleanor denied it. She knew she wasn't wrong. She had seen them together and she had seen the tense, excited look on his face. "What am I going to do?"

Kyria Athena was as bracing as Eleanor had hoped she would be. "You will come to Lindos with us, my dear. And then we'll see!"

Lindos was beautiful. Mrs. Barron had left her cousin Melanie to go on to their relatives alone while she and Eleanor walked through the narrow, cobbled streets that were empty of any traffic except the occasional donkey, making their way slowly towards the famous acropolis that stood high above the rows of square little white houses below in typically Greek confusion.

"I am getting old," Kyria Athena complained as they climbed steadily higher and higher, pausing only to admire what was reputed to be the oldest house in the town. "I get breathless easily these days. When I was young, I would be up and down here twice each day, and I thought nothing of it! Now, I ache in every joint!"

"Perhaps you shouldn't have come?" Eleanor answered, concerned lest her grandmother really was attempting too much.

"You needn't think I'm going all the way!" Kyria Athena panted. "I shall go up to the castle, but not a step further. I'll sit there by the sculptured ship until you come down again. There's no need to hurry. Take your time, my dear. There's a ruined temple dedicated to the goddess Athena up there. I have always found it helpful in times of trouble to stay quite still in some beautiful place and let the atmosphere sink into my very being. You may find things are not nearly as bad as you think now if you do that. Did you spend the whole night alone?"

Eleanor's face burned scarlet as she remembered Ioannis' masterful treatment of her, from the moment he had broken down her door to the time he had given, and received back again from her, a happiness she had not known it was possible to experience. And he had been tinged by that glory too! That she knew, as surely as she knew of her own love for him.

"Well, there you are, my dear!" Kyria Athena went on smoothly. "That must mean something surely?"

Some elderly women, adept in the arts of embroidery, had set up their stalls high up on the hillside, spreading their tablecloths and mats of tatting, their aprons and traycloths, on the outcrops of rock to which the path up the acropolis clung, now that they had left the town behind them. They greeted Kyria Athena like a long-lost sister, laughing at the agony of her expression as she forced herself onwards and teasing her about the soft life she had led while she had been away in England.

Then suddenly the castle came into view, a single flight of steps leading up to it, at the bottom of which was the famous monument of the sculptured ship.

"Are you sure you'll be all right here?" Eleanor felt bound to ask, her foot already poised over the bottom step of the flight up to the castle entrance.

"Better than I would be if I came any further!" her grandmother groaned. "Get along with you, child!"

Eleanor needed no second invitation. She ran lightly up the steps and walked through the mysterious remains of the Knights of St. John's fortifications of the ancient site. Beyond, she could see the ruins of the older temple and its associate buildings, and she went through the dark rooms of the garrison as quickly as she could, gasping with delight when she saw the blue of the sea far, far down below and the elegant remaining columns that reached up into the clear blue of the sky.

It was hot at the very top of the hill. The sun beat down strongly and was reflected by the glare from the ancient stones. Eleanor sat down on a fallen piece of masonry inside the temple itself and looked about her. From where she was she had a bird's-eye view of the whole of Lindos, from the distinctive dome of the whitewashed church, almost lost amongst the crowded houses that clustered about it, to the ancient harbour of St. Paul's, way down below and with only the narrowest outlet to the sea. A more modern harbour lay on the other side, where some sailing boats were racing, skimming before the wind. She watched one of them come to grief in the treacherous waters where a finger of land pointed out into the sea.

Athena, the goddess, had been well-served by her devotees when they had chosen this site for her. Eleanor wondered if Athena had granted them some small part of her wisdom in exchange. She felt as though she could use some now. She sighed.

Suddenly, she was conscious of a presence behind her. She turned round to see Ioannis coming towards her, both hands outstretched. As though in answer to her unspoken thoughts, he said softly, "Has Athena granted you at last a little wisdom? Too bad she wasn't around when you fled our home! Why didn't you stay there and wait for me?"

She put her hands in his. "I thought you'd decided you preferred Mercedes," she said simply. "Are you sure you don't?"

His hands tightened on hers. "Perhaps we both have need of greater wisdom, *agapí mou*. Shall I tell you all about it, here, in the shadow of Athena, and then shall we go home together with her blessings on our heads?"

Eleanor nodded her head, her eyes wide. "Yes, please," she said.

Chapter Eleven

The Temple of Athena at Lindos was a comparatively small building, erected in a deliberately severe style. By 340 B.C. it was already standing high above the town, and it was not the first temple to occupy the site. Before it an earlier building had been created in the Ionic style, the last of the three classical orders of architecture. The present temple had returned to the simplicity of the earliest style of all, the Doric order, which allowed very little decoration of any kind. Perhaps because of this, it marvellously suited the high promontory of land it had been designed to occupy. Clearly visible from the town below, it was permeated with the awed wonder with which the ancient Greeks had revered their gods and goddesses. Some of the reverence remained, and Eleanor felt it very closely as Ioannis sat on the step beside her, his arm about her waist, nipping her closely in beside him.

She found she had nothing to say to him, search her mind as she might. She was content just to be there with him and to know that he had come to seek her out without any prompting from her, because—though she hardly dared to believe it—he had wanted to be with her.

He put a hand on either side of her face, forcing her to look straight back at him. His expression was strangely gentle.

"I haven't been as kind to you as I might have been, have I?" he said.

"I'm not complaining," she answered him. "It can't have been easy for you either. I wish—" What did she wish? She wished he loved her with the same fervour as she did him. But she could hardly tell him that. She put her own hands over his. "We can't stay very long," she told him. "Grandma is waiting down by the sculptured ship. I—I came with her, you see." She gave him a shy look. "How did you know I was here?"

"I didn't. I searched several other places first, most of them a little nearer home. I was afraid you'd hitched a ride again and I wanted you to be with me! I went to Kamiros and Ialysos, even into the old city of Rhodes, but you weren't anywhere to be seen!"

Her lips trembled beneath his gaze. "I wish I'd waited for you! It would have saved you a great deal of trouble, wouldn't it?"

"I don't mind the trouble, sweetheart, as long as you are safe—and not unhappy. I hoped to get back before you woke up!"

She blinked, no longer caring if he should see the misery his absence had caused her. "I thought you might have gone for good."

His mouth tightened. "Never that! Never think anything like that again, because I don't think I could bear it if you did!"

She searched his face with anxious eyes. "It doesn't matter!" she assured him.

"To whom? To you, or to me? Eleanor, don't you know yet that I can't do without you?"

She had no answer to that. She freed herself from his restraining hands and stood up. "Grandma—"

Ioannis stood up also, catching her by the shoulders and turning her round to face him. His expression was decidedly quizzical as he watched her trying to win her freedom by levering up his fingers one by one.

"I could have kissed Kyria Athena when I saw her sitting by the sculptured ship! It hadn't occurred to me before that you would have run straight to her, though I should have known, shouldn't I? She sent me up here to you, *yinéka mou*. Won't you listen to what I have to say?"

She tried to put him off with a platitude, but none would come to mind. "What about Mercedes?" she burst out.

"Ah, that's better!" he commended her. "Now you

sound much more like the jealous shrew I've come to know! What about Mercedes?"

"She's always there!" she complained. "I can't help being jealous of her, Ioannis. Perhaps I wouldn't be if I liked her a bit more, but I don't. I don't like her at all! I wish you didn't!" Her voice quavered and broke and she hid her face against his shoulder. "I want you to like *me!*"

"Do you, sweetheart? Why?"

She shrugged her shoulders. "Most people like their wives, even if they can't love them. Otherwise why do they marry them?"

"Are you asking me why I married you?"

She nodded, unable to answer him properly.

"I didn't mean to at the beginning," he told her, thus shocking her into a new awareness of him. "In fact I didn't mean to stay in Rhodes longer than a few hours when I sailed in that afternoon. It all goes back to my father—"

"Your father?"

"He ran the business before I took over from him. His business sense is only average, however, and he took on someone to help him with the day-to-day matters. That someone was Mercedes' father. He had all the ambition my father lacked, but he could never do all the things he wanted, for, come what may, the firm belonged to my father and not to him. He began to talk about a possible marriage between myself and Mercedes, but my father rejected the match out of hand, as I did myself."

"You made her your mistress instead!" Eleanor put in bitterly.

"I took what was offered to me," he admitted, "but it was not much to my taste. She is good at her job though and, when she was asked to go to Rhodes, I endorsed the idea. There was some likelihood of my spending my holidays in Rhodes, as I have done in previous years, and so she came, a little too pleased perhaps by the way things were turning out between us."

"I'm not surprised. She must have known you loved her!"

"There was no love between us." He could hardly have been more definite about it and Eleanor wondered if she could believe him. But, if it had not been love, why should he have wanted the Greek girl? "We made use of each other," he went on, reading her mind with an exactitude she had noticed before, "but there was no love."

"Oh," she said weakly.

"That is not to say it wouldn't have suited Mercedes almost as much as it would have suited her father if I had married her, but that I shall never do. I have a wife who suits me very well and I want none other! Won't you believe that?"

Eleanor bit her lip. "Does Mercedes believe it?"

"She does now! She won't hurt you again, darling. I promise you that!"

Eleanor's eyes widened. "What did you do to her?" A new anxiety coloured her voice and was only dispelled when he laughed and kissed her briefly on the lips.

"I may have wanted to murder her, for yesterday alone, and for other things too, but I didn't have to be half as drastic as that. She knew the moment she set eyes on me that it was all over between us. She admitted as much. 'Your English wife has won, hasn't she?' she said. 'I never thought she would. I never thought you'd trust your happiness to anyone else but yourself. What has she got that I haven't?'"

"Not very much," Eleanor said. She stirred against him, quite unable to resist asking him, "Was she right, Ioannis? Have you entrusted your happiness to me?"

"I did from the first moment I saw you," he answered. "Didn't you guess?"

She shook her head. "I didn't understand anything!" she declared. "I still don't! Why did you come to Rhodes at all, if not to see Mercedes?"

"I came to see your grandmother. The older generation is very conservative in Greece. My father may not have looked favourably on a marriage between Mercedes and myself, but when your uncle approached him, he reacted as the true Rhodian he is! There was nothing he wanted better than a link between your family and mine! He remembered your grandmother well and in your great-uncle he found a kindred spirit he could not resist. It was some weeks, though, before he could bring himself to tell me he had agreed with the old man that we should be wed. One week before I came to Rhodes I didn't even know of your existence! But I thought it a simple matter to sail across to the old house during my holidays and tell Kyria Athena that it wasn't on, that whatever my father may have agreed with her, I fully intended choosing my own bride in my own time!"

"But you didn't do that?"

"I met you," he said.

She gave him a shattered look. "But you didn't even like me!"

"Didn't I? I wasted a great deal of time on someone I didn't like if that was the case!"

"And you must have known that I didn't like you!" she added forcefully, once again beginning to feel extremely ill-used.

"I thought I could change your mind," he answered, amused. "I planned to plant the suggestion that you might love me so deep in your heart and mind you would never get it out again. I succeeded too! You would never have married me disliking me, would you, Eleanor?"

"I didn't mean to marry you at all! Only, it was just as they always say, that if you hesitate you're lost! I hesitate all the time!"

"But you don't," he said very gently, "not with me. You've never hesitated at all! You meant to attract me from the very beginning, *agapí mou,* if not by wearing your sister's swimming suit, by making it obvious that you needed a strong man to look after you. The implication was irresistible! Naturally I was determined that that man should be me! I made up my mind then and there to marry you as quickly as I could! I had an able ally in the Kyria Athena, but it would have made no difference had she been against the match for you. You are my woman! The only one I want, and the one I mean to have by my side for the rest of my life!"

Had it really been like that? Eleanor tried to concentrate but all common sense seemed to be slipping away from her, leaving a residue of sheer happiness that welled up inside her and cast a glow across her features. She pleated the material of his shirt which she found beneath her fingers and then straightened it out again, the colour coming and going in her cheeks.

"Part of me wanted to marry you very much," she admitted. "I felt as though I were housing a traitor inside me, and I thought you might guess and despise me for it."

He laughed. "Did I despise you last night?" he whispered in her ear, laughter in his voice.

His hands stroked her back, descending to her hips and pulling her closer against him. "One taste of your sweetness has only made me want you the more! For me, it was the beautiful ending of an appalling day! I wanted so badly that everything would be perfect for you, my little bride of the sun, and there wasn't a thing that went right for us! You looked lovely at the church, but scared too, and I longed to tell you that you had nothing to be frightened of from me. Then there was that ghastly fiasco instead of the celebration I had wanted to give you!"

"Oh, Ioannis, I'm sorry!" she blurted out. "I thought you didn't care, and I cared so much! I didn't mean to shut you out—not from me!—only from the unhappiness of all that hatred and beastliness."

"Was that all, *agapi?*" His frame trembled against hers. "I didn't want to force you, but I had to have you *then,* to prove to us both that it didn't matter what happened, what we had between us could rise above it all! Will you forgive me?"

"Oh, Ioannis," she moaned. "If I'd known that you

cared, I'd have come running! But I couldn't get it out of my head that you'd be wishing I were Mercedes all the time. Last night, I hated her! I felt quite sick with hate, and it wasn't a very nice feeling. But, later on, nothing mattered but you!" She smiled at him through tears and laughter. "I love you terribly, Ioannis Hyperion Nikkolides. I *need* you, as the earth needs the sun! Laugh all you like, but I felt as though I really were the bride of the sun! I'll never feel any differently, no matter how long I live, so please, love me a little bit too? I mean, if you can't, I shall quite understand, and I want to be your wife anyway——"

"Love you a little, Eleanor *mou?* My darling fool, I love you to distraction! Did you really believe I'd marry you for a museum of a house we weren't going to live in anyway? What a bargain that would have been! I married you because I couldn't help myself! What other reason could I have had?"

Eleanor was at a loss. "You said you wanted sons," she said at last, "and a woman in your house——"

His laughter made her blush and her heart began to hammer within her, recalling other things that had happened last night and which she was beginning to hope might happen between them again.

"A woman who can't cook on an open fire? Who half-starved herself to death before I took pity on her and fed her until her grandmother came to her rescue? A woman who can't even sweep a yard without getting more dirt on her person than she does in the dustpan? My dear Eleanor——"

"A woman nevertheless!" she snapped at him.

"Ah," he murmured, his eyes glinting with an

emotion she had never seen in them before, "now that is a quite different matter! Very much a woman! One, moreover, who came to life in my arms, and that is an experience I plan to repeat very often—with your full consent, of course?"

"I thought you knew," she said. "You *said* you knew! You even made me say it too! You know you can steal the heart from my body and I can't deny you anything. Not that it would do me any good if I did," she added judiciously. "You'd coerce me shamefully and you wouldn't care at all!"

His arms tightened about her. "And you?" he whispered. "Would you care?"

She stood stock still, feeling the warmth of him through the thin material of her shirt, and she loved him with every bit of her. What was her independence worth against that? She had thought it valuable to her, but it faded into insignificance against the prospect of belonging to Ioannis. That was a dream that would never fade! Who wanted to be a woman alone? Her independence could go—and welcome!

"I love you," she said. "I want to be yours. I want that more than anything else in the world!" She smiled slowly, an element of mischief creeping up into her eyes. "I think I can stand a touch of arrogance if it comes from you. You're you, and I don't want to change you, Ioannis. I like you too much the way you are!"

"I only want to look after you, darling," he protested, and then catching her look of complete disbelief, he laughed. "All right, I admit it, woman! I won't be content till I know you to be flesh of my flesh and bone of my bone, as a wife ought to be, giving all your love and loyalty to me alone! I wanted that as soon as I saw you, and I've wanted it ever since! You're a nagging ache in my body and I can only be complete as a man if I know you to be mine, the fountain of love in my home. That is the Greek way of loving, *agapí mou!* I try to remember you are English and brought up to other ways, but I find I can't change my inner belief that where her man goes a woman should follow! Do I ask too much?"

She shook her head, moved unbearably by the depth of his feelings for her. "I must be more Greek than I knew," she answered, "if that is the Greek way. The earth would be a wasteland without the sun, as I would be without you. The earth doesn't tell the sun when to rise and when to set, but welcomes its warmth daily and lives because of it. My fulfillment has to be in you. Grandma tried to tell me that, you know, and she was right. She loved her husband too, you see, and now she is alone, the fruitfulness and the bounty has gone. We were never very kind to her at home. She always seemed awkward and somehow foreign to the rest of us. Can you understand that? Yet she loved me enough to want me to be happy with you, as she was happy with my grandfather. We thought her a fool and that we were the wise ones, but she knew a wisdom that every woman must envy. No wonder Solomon rated wisdom above gold and silver. So do I!"

His kiss was very gentle. "So you listened to both Athenas in the end?"

She was surprised, as she had forgotten they were still within the boundaries of the temple of the grey-eyed goddess of old. Then she laughed, returning her husband's kiss with enthusiasm.

"It's a sacred trust," she said. "When we're both very old, we'll come back here and thank her all over again!" The laughter fell away from her and she tensed her muscles. "Oh, Ioannis! We must thank Grandma too! I'd forgotten all about her! She must be bored stiff, sitting there, waiting for us to go down to her! We must run!"

"You'll have to thank her later, my sweet, though the success of her plans for her favourite granddaughter will probably be thanks enough! I hate to think what would have happened if I had carried out my original intention and refused to wed you. The old man, Kostas, and she would have pursued me the length and breadth of Greece, breathing vengeance no doubt. The Greeks can hate as well as love, and she has the tenacity to do both well! But, when she saw me coming, she told me she would go down into the town and find her cousin Melanie and that we were not to worry about her. She is busy picking up the threads of her life in Rhodes and is content. So she may be, having got her own way in everything she set out to do!"

"But that isn't why she did it," Eleanor objected. "I know she wanted her brother's house to live in, but it wasn't only that! You might not have agreed to her living there—"

"And be haunted by Kostas' ghost for the rest of my life? *Philotimo* is important to every Rhodian, and he meant to take care of his sister as well as his great-niece. He wouldn't have taken it kindly if I had failed him!"

"But he's dead," Eleanor pointed out. "He couldn't have left me the house as my dowry if he were still alive."

Ioannis smiled wryly. "Your dowry was more than a house, my girl! It was your grandmother's happiness and her future care, tying me to my Rhodian heritage for a long time to come! He never approved of my going to Athens, coming back less and less often to see the island of my birth. Now we'll have to come every year, and probably more often than that!"

It was hard for Eleanor to imagine Ioannis anywhere else but in Rhodes. "Do you mind?" she asked him.

He shrugged his shoulders. "I welcome it. If you can learn to cook an eatable meal on an open fire, I shall look forward to our visits and to being alone together in a way we won't be able to be in Athens." He looked down at her. "Now what's the matter?" he enquired, exasperated.

"I'm hungry!" she said. "You had some supper last night, but I didn't. Nor did *I* have any breakfast. I didn't feel like it, I was so miserable when I found you gone. But now I'm simply *starving!* Is there anywhere here where we could eat?"

Chapter Twelve

The closer they got to Athens, the happier Eleanor felt. Contented as a sleepy cat, she offered an idle hand now and then as they sailed slowly across the Aegean towards the mainland of Greece. Her knowledge of sailing was not much greater now than it ever had been, but it made a lovely end to the most wonderful couple of weeks she had ever known. Ioannis berthed the *caique* at one of the marinas along the Apollon Coast between Athens and Sounium and whistled up a chauffeured limousine that was now carrying them rapidly towards the centre of the capital.

Above the city stood the Acropolis, instantly recognisable, and a stark reminder that the comfortable city that clustered round the bottom of the hill on which it stood had a long venerable history unmatched by anywhere else in Europe.

"Your goddess is the patron of Athens too," Ioannis told her, as she leaned forward to see the golden ruins of the Acropolis better.

"Of course!"

"Poseidon once tried to take the city away from her. He sent his sea water into the city and it came up in a spring up by the Parthenon. You can still see it today, and the water is still salt to the taste."

"But Athena kept her hold on the city?"

Ioannis nodded. "She planted an olive tree beside the spring, and the people of the city chose her symbol rather than his. You can't see the actual olive tree, though you could until fairly recently. Now another one has been planted in its place."

The story pleased Eleanor. "I'm glad. Poseidon has his own domain, and very beautiful it is too—it was lovely sailing across, wasn't it?—but Athena is special and I'm glad we can visit her here too."

Ioannis picked up her hand in his. "Athens isn't Rhodes," he began.

She smiled at him. "I may prefer it! Imagine having a proper stove again! I can't wait to see where we're going to live!"

"That's what I'm trying to tell you," he started again. "It's a quite different life from the one we lived on Rhodes."

"You're afraid I won't like it?" she accused him,

complacent in the new contented security he had surrounded her with during their honeymoon. "I shall like anywhere if you are there too!"

He threaded his fingers through hers. "It's more comfortable than the house on Rhodes," he began for the third time, "but it is an apartment, not a house, and I have my offices down below. There are telephones in every room and they ring frequently. If you don't care for living there, we can move out of the city and buy a house for our own use, but it has a certain convenience that I've become accustomed to since I took over the business from my father."

Eleanor looked across at him, sitting beside her on the wide seat at the back of the car. He was wearing a coat and a tie, and his hair was neatly brushed. She would have to get used to sharing him with his work, she thought, and he would have to get used to it too. It was up to her to make it as easy for them both as she could and that she would do. She squeezed his fingers between hers, smiling at him with a new resolution.

"You don't have to worry about me, darling. I shall be busy too, learning Greek and keeping house for you—"

"There's a maid! She speaks some English, and she's a good cook, but she won't like being interfered with."

"No? What's she like?"

"Middle-aged. Gets impatient over nothing and is always threatening to leave! But she suited me when I was on my own. I don't know what she'll be like with another woman in the house."

Eleanor remained calm. "That's my department. If she goes, I promise you you'll hardly notice her departure. I may not have shone in Rhodes, cooking over an open fire, but I'm quite domesticated given the tools I know. In fact, I shall enjoy it. I've always wanted to remove that slur you put on my character when you despised me for not even being able to sweep up the courtyard properly! I shall have a vacuum cleaner and lots of other gadgets, and you, Ioannis Hyperion, will eat your words!"

He was amused. "What kind of gadgets?"

It occurred to her that she had simply no idea what kind of a standard of living her husband maintained. Perhaps he couldn't afford many gadgets?

"I'll make do with a cooker and a vacuum cleaner," she answered at once. "I'm not nearly as spoilt as you think!"

The look on his face made her heart turn over. She had a very good idea of what he was thinking and she wondered herself whether it would be just the same sharing a proper bed with him as it had been on the sleeping platform in the house in Rhodes, the nuptial canopy over their heads, or on the *caique,* with all the stars of heaven to keep them company. There was a lot to be said for the primitive life after all.

The car drew up outside an imposing building of concrete and glass, and the chauffeur opened the door for them to alight, bowing low as they stepped out onto the pavement. Ioannis took her elbow and guided her in through some heavy, self-opening doors and into an exotic, carpeted elevator that bore them swiftly and silently upwards.

As the elevator doors opened again, he took a step towards her and lifted her bodily up into his arms.

"Welcome home, Eleanor *mou!*" he said in her ear, and carried her effortlessly out of the elevator and into the apartment that was to be their home.

Eleanor looked about her with wonder and then she began to laugh. The contrast with his house in Rhodes struck her as peculiarly funny. This was how the rich lived, and it was quite different from the way his peasant forebears, and hers too, had eked out an existence on the island.

"The taps in the bathroom look like gold!" she exclaimed, when she had sufficiently recovered herself to say anything at all.

"They are gold."

"And the sheets are real linen!" She came to an abrupt stop, noticing something else. "Ioannis, they've been embroidered too!"

He came to the door of the bedroom, watching her closely. "The Kyria Athena worked them at the same time she was doing the others."

Eleanor blushed. "It was one of the things I was going to miss," she confessed, averting her face from his gaze. "I liked to see our initials together on the pillow under your head in the morning—*Ioannis?*"

She would never be able to hear him coming across these thick, silky carpets, she thought, abandoning herself to the pressure of his hands. "Ioannis! What about the maid?"

"What about her?" he answered thickly. "I want to see more than an embroidered motif on *my* pillow, *agapí!* You'd better tell me now if you're about to be overcome with hunger? No? How very convenient, because the maid won't be coming in until morning!"

"Ioannis, we *can't!*"

His laughter was so close to her it could have been her own. She held out her arms to him in mute surrender, her breath quickening in time to his.

"Ioannis, I love you so much!"

For a long moment he didn't answer, and then he said, "I love you too, *yinéka mou,* and love you I will whatever the hour of day!"

She ran her fingers through his hair and down the hard, male lines of his back, as willing as he to give way to their mutual desires. Daytime was the time of the sun, and if that was the way he wanted it, that was the way it would be. For she was the bride of Ioannis Hyperion Nikkolides, and therefore the bride of the sun itself! And her last fears left her; rich man or poor man, he was her man and she was forever his, in Athens, in Rhodes, or at the furthest extremities of the earth.

He eased himself up onto his elbows, tracing the line of her cheek with his finger. "What, no arguments, *agapí mou?*"

"None that I can think of," she said with dignity, before she hugged herself closer to him.

"Then, welcome home, my love," he said, as he bent his head to meet her willing lips.

Silhouette Romance

ROMANCE THE WAY
IT USED TO BE...
AND COULD BE AGAIN

*Contemporary romances for today's women
Each month, six very special love stories will
be yours from SILHOUETTE. Look for them
wherever books are sold or order now
from the coupon below.*

$1.50 each

_____ # 1 PAYMENT IN FULL Anne Hampson   (57001-3)
_____ # 2 SHADOW AND SUN Mary Carroll   (57002-1)
_____ # 3 AFFAIRS OF THE HEART Nora Powers   (57003-X)
_____ # 4 STORMY MASQUERADE Anne Hampson (57004-8)
_____ # 5 PATH OF DESIRE Ellen Goforth   (57005-6)
_____ # 6 GOLDEN TIDE Sondra Stanford   (57006-4)
_____ # 7 MIDSUMMER BRIDE Mary Lewis   (57007-2)
_____ # 8 CAPTIVE HEART Patti Beckman   (57008-0)
_____ # 9 WHERE MOUNTAINS WAIT Fran Wilson (57009-9)
_____ #10 BRIDGE OF LOVE Leslie Caine   (57010-2)
_____ #11 AWAKEN THE HEART Dorothy Vernon   (57011-0)
_____ #12 UNREASONABLE SUMMER Dixie Browning

                                                        (57012-9)
_____ #13 PLAYING FOR KEEPS Brooke Hastings (57013-7)
_____ #14 RED, RED ROSE Tess Oliver   (57014-5)
_____ #15 SEA GYPSY Fern Michaels   (57015-3)
_____ #16 SECOND TOMORROW Anne Hampson   (57016-1)
_____ #17 TORMENTING FLAME Nancy John   (57017-X)
_____ #18 THE LION'S SHADOW Elizabeth Hunter (57018-8)
_____ #19 THE HEART NEVER FORGETS Carolyn Thornton

                                                        (57019-6)
_____ #20 ISLAND DESTINY Paula Fulford   (57020-X)
_____ #21 SPRING FIRES Leigh Richards   (57021-8)
_____ #22 MEXICAN NIGHTS Jeanne Stephens   (57022-6)
_____ #23 BEWITCHING GRACE Paula Edwards   (57023-4)

Silhouette Romance

___ #24 SUMMER STORM Letitia Healy (57024-2)
___ #25 SHADOW OF LOVE Sondra Stanford (57025-0)
___ #26 INNOCENT FIRE Brooke Hastings (57026-9)
___ #27 THE DAWN STEALS SOFTLY Anne Hampson
(57027-7)
___ #28 MAN OF THE OUTBACK Anne Hampson (57028-5)
___ #29 RAIN LADY Faye Wildman (57029-3)
___ #30 RETURN ENGAGEMENT Diana Dixon (57030-7)
___ #31 TEMPORARY BRIDE Phyllis Halldorson (57031-5)
___ #32 GOLDEN LASSO Fern Michaels (57032-3)
___ #33 A DIFFERENT DREAM Donna Vitek (57033-1)
___ #34 THE SPANISH HOUSE Nancy John (57034-X)
___ #35 STORM'S END Sondra Stanford (57035-8)
___ #36 BRIDAL TRAP Rena McKay (57036-6)
___ #37 THE BEACHCOMBER Patti Beckman (57037-4)
___ #38 TUMBLED WALL Dixie Browning (57038-2)
___ #39 PARADISE ISLAND Tracy Sinclair (57039-0)
___ #40 WHERE EAGLES NEST Anne Hampson (57040-4)
___ #41 THE SANDS OF TIME Ann Owen (57041-2)
___ #42 DESIGN FOR LOVE Nora Powers (57042-0)
___ #43 SURRENDER IN PARADISE Sandra Robb (57043-9)
___ #44 DESERT FIRE Brooke Hastings (57044-7)
___ #45 TOO SWIFT THE MORNING Mary Carroll (57045-5)
___ #46 NO TRESPASSING Sondra Stanford (57046-3)
___ #47 SHOWERS OF SUNLIGHT Donna Vitek (57047-1)
___ #48 A RACE FOR LOVE Faye Wildman (57048-X)
___ #49 DANCER IN THE SHADOWS Linda Wisdom (57049-8)
___ #50 DUSKY ROSE Joanna Scott (57050-1)
___ #51 BRIDE OF THE SUN Elizabeth Hunter (57051-X)

SILHOUETTE BOOKS, Department SB/1

1230 Avenue of the Americas, New York, N.Y. 10020

Please send me the books I have checked above. I am enclosing $_____
(please add 50¢ to cover postage and handling for each order. N.Y.S. and N.Y.C.
residents please add appropriate sales tax). Send check or money order—no
cash or C.O.D.s please. Allow up to six weeks for delivery.

NAME_____

ADDRESS_____

CITY_____ STATE/ZIP_____

SB/12/80